SPELLBINDING SECRETS

Mystic Inn Mysteries
Book 9

STEPHANIE DAMORE

Chapter 1

"And here are your keys." Our realtor, Tammy Ashford, handed over two gold keys on a single ring. We'd signed our documents earlier that morning at the title company. Tammy met us at our new house as soon as the former owner, Gayle, had signed her portion.

As Vance took the keys from Tammy, I couldn't help but beam with excitement. We'd been house hunting for months, and the journey had been a long one, but now, here we were holding the keys to our very own home. We were fortunate with the location; it was in a quaint neighborhood, not far from the business district, which was convenient to Vance's office and Mystic Inn.

I gazed up at the Victorian-style house, admiring its character. The home was charming, even with the peeling paint. The yard was over-grown and in desperate need of a good trimming too, but the roses along the fence were in full bloom.

"Is everything all set then?" Gayle strolled up the driveway. Her fiery red hair blew behind her despite the scarf tied around her head. The woman might've been past retirement age, but I wouldn't tell her that. She was proud to work for the Agency of Paranormal Particularities, rounding up bad supernaturals all around the world. She'd shared some of her adventures with us the first time we'd met her last week. Gayle inherited the house from her sister, Harriet. The Moonstones had lived in the home for decades until both passed. First Gerald, and then Harriet a few months back. Luckily for us, Gayle hadn't intended to settle down.

"We are. Thank you. We appreciate it." Vance jingled the keys in his hand.

"Wonderful." Gayle clapped her hands. "I'm off to Costa Rica, then. There's a nasty warlock cursing tourists again. They never learn." Gayle rolled her eyes. "But it keeps me young. I'll stop back on my way through next week. The basement's a mess. Sorry about that. Just keep whatever you'd like and toss the rest. ACK!" Gayle jumped back in surprise and had Vance and me reaching for our wands. None of us had seen Rocky sneak up behind the magical bounty hunter. The gargoyle was acting like a curious pooch and caught us off guard.

Gayle shot out a spell quicker than lightning. The curse bounced right off Rocky's concrete-like skin and ricocheted, breaking an upstairs garage window. The two-story, detached garage had enough space to store two cars, plus an upstairs apartment that hadn't been used in years.

Vance and I winced at the sound of glass shattering, but we knew Gayle meant no harm, and neither did Rocky. He was more like a part of the family now, having adopted us since our wedding. With his stocky build, impressive jowls, and large, mighty wings, he might have intimidated some, but to us, he was just a playful and lovable gargoyle.

"It's okay. He's with us," I said a moment too late. "He's just excited to see you."

Rocky, seeming to understand the situation, retreated a few steps and sat down on his haunches next to Vance. He tilted his head to the side and let out a low whine as if apologizing for startling Gayle.

"It's okay, buddy," Vance said, giving him a pat on the head. "No harm done."

Gayle laughed nervously and rubbed her arms, clearly still a bit shaken. "Well, that's a surprise, and very few things surprise me," she said with a smile. "Sorry about the window. Occupational hazard. You have to shoot first and ask questions later if you want to live."

"I can understand that." Both Vance and I were jumpy, given our recent adventures. I couldn't imagine how I'd be after a lifetime of chasing bad guys.

"I'll send someone to take care of it." Gayle motioned to the window. We nodded our appreciation. "Well, I better be off." Gayle shook her head as she looked at Rocky. "I'll see you two next week." With that, she turned on her heel and strode down the driveway, leaving Vance and me alone with Rocky.

I took a deep breath and looked up at Vance. Taking his hand in mine, he said, "Let's go take a look inside."

I smiled, giving him a quick kiss on the cheek. "After you."

We made our way up the front porch, with Rocky following close behind. As we unlocked the front door and stepped inside, I felt a rush of excitement. The house was ours, and we had a whole new life ahead of us.

As if sensing my excitement, Rocky let out a happy bark and bounded into the living room. Vance and I followed, taking in our new surroundings. Every time I walked through the front door, I was struck by the beauty of the entryway. A second oversized door separated the house from the mud room. Once inside, intricate molding adorned every inch of the walls. The living room, which lay just to the left, was filled with light thanks to the floor-to-ceiling windows looking out onto the side garden. A marble fireplace served as the room's centerpiece.

To the right of the entryway was the formal dining room. A beautiful, albeit dusty, chandelier hung from the center of the ceiling. At night, it would bathe the room in warm light while the windows looked out onto the front porch.

Moving further into the house was the kitchen. This was the one room that had been updated. A large island in the center of the room provided plenty of workspace. A white farmhouse sink and stainless-steel appliances took up the perimeter, making the layout perfect. A wall of windows and the backdoor looked out into the yard. All that was missing out back was a deck and a grill.

Back in the entryway, a grand staircase led to the second floor. Upstairs, there were three bedrooms. The master bedroom was imposing, with its high ceilings and oversized windows. The ensuite bathroom featured a beautiful clawfoot tub, perfect for soaking in after a long day.

The first time we walked into the house, I thought this was a home built to last. From the intricate moldings to the marble fireplace and the custom woodwork, the level of craftsmanship was inspiring, even if the inspector said we'd have to replace the wiring sooner rather than later. Despite the work that needed to be done, I was excited about the possibilities and grateful for the chance to call it our own.

Vance and I were back at his truck after surveying inside. Even though Harriet had passed away a couple of months ago, she'd lived in an assisted living facility prior, leaving the house empty for the better part of a year. It was probably longer than that, based on the dust collected on the windowsills and the cobwebs in the corners. Vance and I had planned on cleaning the house and painting the living room before moving in this weekend, but now that seemed rather ambitious.

"Where do you want to start?" Vance asked.

"Do you want to tackle the bathrooms, and I'll start in the kitchen?" I bought new shelf liners to cut for the kitchen drawers and cabinets after cleaning them.

"Helllooo!" my aunt's high-pitched voice called out. I turned around to see Aunt Thelma and Clemmie marching up the driveway.

"We're here to help. Just point us in the right direction!" Clemmie clapped, adding to the enthusiasm.

"I'll bet you two dollars she sends you to work outside," Aunt Thelma told her friend.

"She better not. Who knows what's living in those bushes?"

"But you have such a lovely garden," my aunt started to say.

"Doesn't mean I want to go digging in hers," Clemmie grumbled.

I interrupted the duo. "You guys don't have to help."

"Oh, hush now. What else do we have to do?" Aunt Thelma asked.

Seeing that both women were business owners, probably plenty.

"The inn is a well-oiled machine, and the tea shop is closed for the day. We are all yours." Aunt Thelma whipped her wand out of her back pocket.

"Hey, you found it." The last time I talked to my aunt, she didn't know where she had placed her wand yet again. For once, it wasn't in the teapot.

"It had rolled right under my bed. Can you believe that? A summoning charm found it in no time."

Vance got us down to business. "Angie and I were coming up with a plan. I think she said something about taking the kitchen, and I'm going to head to the bathroom."

"I'll come with you. I have a spell that destroys soap scum in a snap." Clemmie winked.

"And I'll help you in the kitchen," Aunt Thelma nodded.

It was settled. We paired off two by two and got to work.

As Clemmie and Vance went upstairs to tackle the bathrooms, Aunt Thelma and I went to work in the kitchen. I was in the middle of wiping down the counters when I heard a shriek.

"EEEEEEE! It's going to get me!" Clemmie screamed.

Aunt Thelma and I ran out of the kitchen. I raced around the corner and looked up the stairs. A red squirrel stared back at me from the top of the banister. Its eyes were bright and curious, scanning the room as it tried to assess the situation. Its little nose twitched rapidly, taking in the scents and sounds of its new surroundings.

"Rocky, no!" Vance shouted as the gargoyle pranced at the bottom of the stairs. I went to reach for his collar, but I was too late. Rocky tore up the stairs.

"Rocky!" I hollered after him.

With a flick of its tail, the squirrel dashed to the left, then darted to the right trying to outmaneuver Rocky, before flying off the rail and onto the floor.

"Hey, now!" Clemmie shouted as Rocky almost knocked her over as he tore past. "You're going to make me break a hip!"

"Rocky, stop!" Vance's commanding voice rang out.

Rocky didn't listen and continued chasing the squirrel around the upstairs hallway. Clemmie and Vance stepped back into the bathroom to get out of the way. Rocky, caught up in the excitement of the chase, dug his nails into the floor, gauging the hard-wood. The agile and nimble squirrel evaded Rocky's grasp with ease.

I could've transformed into a cat and attempted to catch the squirrel, but with my luck, Rocky would come after me, and I wasn't sure how many of my nine lives I'd already used up.

"I'll get him!" Clemmie shouted as she popped back out of the bathroom with her wand at the ready. She trained her wand at the squirrel and shot off a freezing spell. "Glacio!" Blue light blasted out of the tip of her wand, but the squirrel outsmarted her. A large patch of ice appeared on the opposite wall.

The squirrel turned tail, jumped onto the banis-ter, and ran down the length a bit before flying off the railing and running right between Clemmie's legs and into the guest bedroom.

"ROFF! ROFF! ROFF!" Rocky barked in hot pursuit.

Clemmie and Vance took off after them. Aunt Thelma and I weren't far behind as we thundered up the stairs.

"Where did he go?" I looked around the mostly empty room. The former owners had left a bit of furniture behind both downstairs and up here, but not enough for the squirrel to seemingly disappear into.

"He couldn't have vanished." Aunt Thelma had her hands on her hips as she surveyed the space.

Rocky walked around with his nose to the ground, trying to sniff the intruder out.

"He must've gone out the window," Vance commented. The window was cracked a couple of inches to help air out the house. I didn't think it was enough for a squirrel to fit through, but it must've been.

"He couldn't fit through there," Clemmie said, reading my thoughts.

"I don't know. I guess it's a mystery." I shrugged.

"At least it's not a dead body." Clemmie nodded her head knowingly.

"This is true," I remarked. We'd had enough of those.

After searching a bit more, we still came up empty.

Aunt Thelma clapped her hands. "Okay, guess it's back to work then."

"Hello?" Vance's mom's voice rang through the empty house. "You guys here?"

"Upstairs," Vance shouted back as we exited the guest room.

"Rogue squirrel," Clemmie explained as we followed one another down the stairs.

"What's this about a squirrel?" Heather asked.

"It's nothing, hopefully," I added.

"I brought you guys some food. Thought you

might be hungry. There's plenty for everyone," Heather offered.

We followed Vance's mom into the kitchen. She had two brown paper bags full of takeout containers from the diner she owned.

The tantalizing smell of freshly cooked food filled the kitchen as Heather unpacked the bags. "I brought a chef's salad with avocado ranch dressing, two club sandwiches, macaroni and cheese, and Angie's Monte Cristo sandwich." My mother-in-law winked at me. She knew it was my favorite. "I've also got a peach cobbler and a pint of vanilla ice cream for dessert. Is the freezer working?"

"I think so. I just want to wipe everything down first," I explained.

Heather opened the food containers. The chef's salad was a work of art with crisp lettuce leaves, cherry tomatoes, sliced cucumbers, hard-boiled eggs, diced ham, and shredded cheese, all perfectly arranged in a large bowl. The club sandwich was stacked high with layers of turkey, bacon, lettuce, tomato, and mayonnaise, all held together with toothpicks. The Monte Cristo sandwich was a crispy, golden-brown delight filled with sliced ham, turkey, and Swiss cheese and served with raspberry jam. Don't even get me started on Heather's home-made mac and cheese. My mother-in-law might love me, but even she wouldn't part with her recipe.

As for the peach cobbler, it was a sight to

behold. The golden-brown crust was sprinkled with sugar, and the filling bubbled with fresh, juicy peaches. Heather scooped a generous serving into a bowl and topped it with a scoop of vanilla ice cream, letting it melt and pool around the edges of the warm cobbler.

My mouth watered as Heather passed the plates around the table. We all dug in eagerly, savoring each delicious bite.

In no time, we put a dent in the food, and with my belly full, I was more prone to take a nap than get back to work. I eyed the refrigerator. I really did want to give it a good wipe-down before filling it with food.

Aunt Thelma read my mind. "Here, let me do it."

I was grateful for Aunt Thelma's offer. Cleaning the refrigerator was the last thing I wanted to do, but it needed to be done. My aunt pointed her wand at the fridge and whispered a spell. Suddenly, the refrigerator shrunk down to a quarter of its original size. Vance and I pulled it forward to clean behind it while Aunt Thelma filled the kitchen sink with soapy water.

Dust, old papers, and what looked like a few dead bugs were behind the fridge.

"Look at this. It's an old calendar from 1996." Vance held up the faded, spiral-bound paper.

Appointments and birthdays had been written in a neat script on the dates. We also found more papers, including old bills and a plastic placemat. Vance went to find a broom and dustpan while I continued to sift through the documents, stopping on a note.

"What's this?" My brow furrowed as I read, "Lulu will never forgive me if I confess, but I don't know if I can live with this secret."

"Who's Lulu?" Clemmie asked, coming over and reading over my shoulder.

"Come again?" Aunt Thelma turned the kitchen faucet off.

I reread the note.

"I don't know any Lulu, do you?" Aunt Thelma looked at Clemmie and then Heather. As lifelong residents of Silverlake, the trio knew just about everyone.

"Beats me," Clemmie replied.

"I haven't a clue," Heather added.

"Huh." I turned the paper over in my hand.

"Is there a date or anything?" Vance asked.

"No, but it looks like it was torn out of something." I held up the jagged edges for the group to see. "Do you think it's Harriet's writing?"

"It must be, don't you think?" Heather replied.

I rifled through the rest of the papers, but there wasn't anything else noteworthy.

"This house seems right up your alley. First, a

disappearing squirrel, and now a mysterious note. This house suits you." Clemmie smirked.

"Gee, thanks." I sighed and shook my head, folding the note and pocketing it. There'd be plenty of time to think about what secrets Harriet was keeping *after* we moved in.

Chapter 2

The following day, Clemmie, and our friend Diane, who owned La Luna bakery, met at Spellbinding Books. The two-story bookstore was a charming sight. It was one of those bookstores that could steal hours out of your day without you even realizing it. Stepping inside, I was greeted with the warm scent of aged paper and leather bindings. Customers could enter from either side, but I preferred the back entrance. It was flanked by two factory-sized windows that let in abundant sunshine and ample reading light. Beyond the windows was a rear patio with wrought iron tables and chairs arranged invitingly. It was the perfect place to enjoy a coffee or tea and continue reading in the fresh air.

My best friend Misty owned the bookstore, and today we had a very special event to plan. Next month was Aunt Thelma's 70th birthday, and we wanted to make it memorable. The woman didn't look near her age, though, thanks to the glamour lotions and spells she dabbled with. If she kept it up, she'd start looking younger than me.

"How about we hire a couple of hot men wearing nothing but bowties and top hats?" Clemmie wiggled her eyebrows.

"Ew." I scrunched my face.

"How about no?" Misty replied on my behalf.

"Maybe something more low-key? Like an afternoon tea at your shop?" Diane suggested.

"No, no. We need something fun, something with a little pizzazz." Clemmie added jazz hands to her statement.

Our group was silent while we tried to come up with something else.

Misty spoke up. "How about the roller rink?"

"What is it with you youngin's trying to get me to break my hip? If it's not Rocky barreling toward me, it's roller skating," Clemmie quipped. "It's all fun when you're a kid, but if you fall and break something when you're old, it's the beginning of the end, I tell you, magic or not."

"Okay, fine. No broken hips," Misty agreed.

"We could plan a ball. You know…" I snapped my fingers, trying to think of the words. "Like in those historical romance novels she loves." Aunt Thelma was always preordering a romance novel from Misty. She could always prepay and conjure the book on release day, but she liked giving Misty the business. Plus, it gave me an extra excuse to stop in and chat with Misty. I wasn't complaining.

Clemmie's eyes lit up. "Yes! A ball. That's perfect. We could have live music; a ton of flowers," Clemmie looked knowingly at Diane. Her husband owned the flower shop.

"Don't forget the food," Misty added.

"Ooh, I know. We could serve those little finger sandwiches, maybe shrimp cocktail, and crostinis topped with prosciutto and goat cheese," Diane started to say.

"And champagne," Misty added.

I started writing everything down.

"Don't forget the cake." Diane tapped on the corner of my paper.

"Of course. We'll put you in charge of that," I replied, adding it to the list.

Diane beamed with excitement. "Oh, this sounds lovely. I've always wanted to attend a ball."

"But where would we hold it?" I wondered. The inn was my first thought, but I wanted this to be special, and I wasn't sure the family business was the right venue.

Diane spoke up. "What about the community center? They have a large ballroom with a stage and a beautiful chandelier. I know the manager there, and I could talk to her about renting it out."

Clemmie clapped her hands. "It's settled then. We'll plan a ball for Thelma's platinum jubilee."

"Platinum jubilee?" I asked.

"If the Queen of England can have one, so can Thelma," Clemmie added.

"I'd say she's ruled Silverlake for the past seventy years," Diane agreed.

"Don't let Mayor Parish hear you say that," Misty added.

Clemmie ignored her and continued. "I'll take care of the orchestra. We'll put Roger in charge of the flowers. Misty can handle the food, and Diane will handle the venue and cake. Angelica, you tackle the invitations and coordinate everything. You good with that?"

I nodded. "I'm thinking we'll do calligraphy invitations?" It seemed like the style would fit in with a regency ball. At least, it did in my mind.

"That would be perfect," Misty agreed.

"Okay, good." I'd have to find someone to handle the invitations. I had decent penmanship, but calligraphy wasn't my forté.

We spent the next hour planning every detail, from the color scheme to the guest list, before Clemmie brought up the note I found behind the fridge.

"You uncovered another mystery?" Diane asked as we all stood to leave.

"I guess. I'm not sure how I'd ever solve it or if it's even worth it to snoop around," I confessed.

"You know who might know about Lulu?" Diane started to say.

"Who?" Misty asked.

"Mrs. Potts. She's about Harriet's age. I used to see them playing cards together at the senior center when I'd deliver cookies now and again."

"I should've thought of that," Clemmie spoke up. "Those two ladies were friends, weren't they?" she said more to herself than anyone.

"Huh, maybe I'll ask her about it next time I see her," I replied.

"Let us know what you find out. Now, if you don't mind, I've got to scoot. I have a hot date tonight." Clemmie went to walk away.

"Hold up! You can't drop that and leave," Misty moved to stop Clemmie.

"Yeah, who are you dating?" I asked, catching Diane's eye. She shook her head. Diane had no idea, either.

"Guess I shouldn't call it a date. We're just having ourselves a little chat over the computer," Clemmie clarified.

"You're online dating?" Misty looked incredulous.

"Don't look at me that way," Clemmie replied defensively.

"What are you talking about? You're the one

who cursed your cell phone when it told you your voicemail was full!" Misty shot back.

Diane and I laughed. Clemmie's poor phone never worked the same again. She eventually had to get a new one.

"That was months ago. Besides, I have to do something. You all are pairing off like geese, or is it swans? You know, whatever birds it is that pair up for life. I'm not getting any younger. I need to get in on the action. Now, excuse me. I need to get to gettin'." Clemmie nodded her goodbye and wasted no time heading out.

"Sometimes, I worry about her," Misty confessed.

"I know me too." I loved Clemmie. There wasn't anything I wouldn't do for her or my aunt. I only hoped she knew what she was doing with the online dating bit. Even I wasn't crazy enough to enter those waters when I was single. There might be plenty of fish in the sea, but there were plenty of slimy goblin sharks too.

Chapter 3

Just as we were leaving the bookstore, my phone rang. It was Vance. "Hey, we have a bit of an emergency at the house," he said, sounding out of breath.

"What's going on?" My mind raced with everything that could go wrong.

"A pipe broke in the basement. Water sprayed everywhere. I turned off the main valve, but not before the basement flooded."

"Are you okay? Is there a lot of damage?"

"I'm fine, but the water has soaked through the floor. Some of the boxes left here are ruined."

"Oh no. I hope Gayle didn't leave anything important behind."

"Yeah, not sure. We'll have to get the boxes out and rip up the carpet. But first, we need a plumber."

I took a deep breath, trying to remain calm. "Okay, I'll start making some calls and head your way."

I turned to my friends, who had been listening to my side of the conversation. "We have a bit of a situation. I need to find a plumber and get back to the house. Vance says a pipe burst in the basement, and there's water everywhere."

"I know someone," Diane offered, digging in her purse and pulling out her phone. "I can call him and see if he can swing by. Is that okay?"

"That would be perfect."

"I'll text you and tell you what he says," Diane added.

"Thank you. I'll catch up with you guys later." I waved goodbye and headed right home.

As I made the quick trip, I thought briefly about the mystery note. I wondered what it could be about and if it was worth uncovering. After all, Vance and I had our hands full with the new house, but I didn't want to let it go entirely. I decided to ask Mrs. Potts about Harriet the next time I saw her. Until then, my focus was on turning our new house into a home.

Back at the house, I descended the steps to the dark and dank basement. The only light source came from a single bulb hanging from the ceiling. Vance was right; the basement was a mess. The old brown carpet smelled musty, and the standing water seeped into the bottom boxes. The rest of the base-ment was empty except for our furnace and an old refrigerator tucked away in the corner.

Vance was standing next to the furnace with a look of concern on his face.

"How bad is it?" I asked.

"Not sure. We need to call an HVAC guy." Vance bent low and used the light from his phone to look closer. The furnace had already taken on some water. I could hear the motor whirring in a strained sort of way. I hoped it wasn't broken beyond repair. Good thing it wasn't winter. The nights were still in the fifties, but that was better than below-freezing.

"I'll see if Diane knows someone." I took out my phone. Diane had already texted me. I read her message and then shot off a quick text to ask about an HVAC recommendation. "She already has a plumber headed here."

"Hey, guys, we're here," Misty called from the top of the stairs.

I looked over my shoulder and saw her and her boyfriend, Daniel. "I thought you had to stay at the store?" When we parted, Misty still had a couple more hours left of her shift.

"I called Vicky and filled her in. She offered to come in."

Daniel and Misty had come prepared, wearing rain boots that came up past their shins. I was still standing on the bottom basement step, observing from afar.

Misty stepped down to me and gave me a side hug. "How bad is it?"

"That's what I just asked. We're not sure yet. We're worried about the furnace."

Misty winced. Everyone knew furnaces weren't cheap.

"Any idea how it happened?" Daniel asked, stepping into the water.

"Not a clue. The pipes are pretty old. Maybe one just gave out? The plumber should be here shortly," I answered.

Daniel rolled up his sleeves and took a few steps forward. "Alright then. Where should we start?"

I pointed to the boxes. "If we can get these out of here, we can start pulling up the carpet."

Misty nodded. "Got it."

"I'm going to conjure a pair of boots, and then I'll join you," I said.

It took some time, but between the four of us, we managed to move all the boxes upstairs into the garage. Then Vance and Daniel worked on ripping up the old, waterlogged carpet while Misty and I cast drying spells on the concrete.

The plumber arrived amid the cleanup and confirmed what we'd suspected—the pipes were old, and several of the fittings needed to be replaced. After taking a look at the extent of the damage, he told us he'd be back in an hour to start the work.

"Whew." Misty wiped the sweat from her brow. "I don't know about you guys, but I could use a break."

I rubbed my temples. "I think we all could."

Vance stood up, stretching his back. "You guys want to head up?"

"Sure," Misty said, and Daniel nodded.

I blinked into the bright sunlight. It was hard to believe it was still afternoon. It felt like we'd worked the entire day. I was starving. "How about I order pizza?"

"Sounds good to me," Misty replied.

"How does everyone feel about pepperoni?" I asked.

"I'll eat anything," Daniel replied.

"I'm with Daniel," Vance agreed.

I laughed. "I guess we're all starving."

After calling in the pizza, Misty and I walked outside toward the garden, taking in the overgrown grass and the wildflowers while the guys toured the inside. I spotted an old wooden swing that had seen better days, and Misty made a beeline for it.

"Careful, the wood might be rotten," I warned as she plopped down on the creaky seat.

"Oh, come on. Live a little," Misty teased. I hesitated momentarily before joining her. Thankfully, the swing held our weight. "Your yard has so much potential," she said, looking out at the over-grown garden. "You could turn it into a little oasis."

I nodded in agreement, admiring her optimism. "It's going to take a lot of work, though."

Misty grinned. "We've never been afraid of hard work. Remember when we painted my entire apartment that one weekend?"

"Oh my goodness, that color!" I cringed, remembering the bright green paint.

"It was called limeade, if I recall," Misty pushed off the ground, and the swing rocked back.

"What had we been thinking?"

"I have no idea."

"Thankfully, our style sense has evolved over the years."

"This is true."

I leaned back, feeling the breeze on my face. For a moment, I forgot about the plumbing and heating problems. The swing creaked back and forth, and I closed my eyes, imagining what the garden could look like with a bit of love and attention.

Chapter 4

Rocky barreled through the rose bushes and brought me out of my daydream.

"What are you doing?" I asked the hyped-up gargoyle.

Rocky was going crazy, scratching and digging in the overgrown flower bed.

"Is it that darn squirrel again?" I stood up and tried to get a closer look. "Come on, Rocky. Get out of there." For all I knew, the flowerbed was over-grown with poison ivy, or what if there was a ground hornet nest or something? I wasn't sure if gargoyles were affected by either, and I didn't want to find out.

I reached down to grab Rocky's collar and pull him back. It was like trying to move a boulder. Rocky continued to dig and throw dirt everywhere, ignoring my commands. Clumps of dirt pelted my legs.

It wasn't until I grunted and pulled with all my might that Rocky finally relented. He turned around and dropped something at my feet.

At first, I couldn't make out what it was. It looked like a tree root covered in dirt. But upon closer inspection, I realized they were bones. Worse, it was a human hand. "Oh no." I stumbled back.

"What in the world?" Misty rushed over.

Rocky barked excitedly, his tail wagging as if he had just found the greatest treasure in the world.

"A hand?" Misty whispered as she stepped beside me.

I nodded mutely, still trying to process what had just happened. The joints were caked in soil as if they had been buried long ago. The skin and tissue were long gone.

"I think you uncovered Harriet's secret," Misty said grimly.

I swallowed the lump stuck in my throat. "I think you're right." The cryptic note plus the bones seemed too much of a coincidence.

My heart thumped uncomfortably as I stared down at the skeletal hand. I knew what to do but didn't want to do it. We'd officially owned our house for one day, and I had already uncovered a dead body, or part of one anyway. That had to be some sort of record. Now, our brand-new home was going to become a crime scene.

Rocky went back to digging at the remains. "Run and grab the guys, would you?" Vance would have better luck controlling Rocky. "I'll call this in."

I dialed the sheriff's department and was greeted by Dottie's cheerful voice. Dottie had lived in Silverlake for just over a year. The jolly woman from the Midwest became more talkative with every phone call.

"Good morning, Sheriff's department. How can I help you?"

"Hi, Dottie. This is Angelica Blackwell."

"Deputy Blackwell! Oh, how lovely to hear from you. How's married life treating you? I just loved your wedding. An outdoor winter ceremony, who would have thought of it? Your aunt is a clever woman."

"Thanks, Dottie. Listen, I think we have a situation here at the new house. Is Sheriff Reynolds in?"

"Oh no, what happened?"

I didn't want word to get around too fast, but I knew there was no point in keeping everything under wraps. Gossip flew faster than spells in Silverlake. "Rocky just dug up a human hand in my flowerbed, a skeleton one. I'm not sure if there are more remains." I let my voice trail off.

"Oh my gosh, honey. Are you okay?" she exclaimed.

"I'm fine. Just a little shaken up," I tried to keep my voice even.

"Of course you are. It's okay to be shaken up. Let me get you to the right people. We'll send some deputies over right away."

"Thank you," I exhaled and was ready to hang up, but Dottie kept talking.

"Are you enjoying your new home, then?" Her tone was upbeat.

"It's, uh, it's been eventful." I glanced down at the bones.

"I bet. You must be so excited to start this new chapter in your life. I remember when my husband and I bought our first home. It was such a special time," she continued.

"It is. It was," I said; my mind preoccupied with the situation.

"What kind of home did you buy?" Dottie pressed on.

"It's a Victorian." I kept my answers brief, trying to cut the conversation short.

"Oh, I love Victorians! They're so charming. You know, I've always wanted to live in a Victorian. I bet it's beautiful," she gushed.

"It is, but we've got a lot of work to do."

"Well, that's the fun part, isn't it? Making it your own."

"About those deputies?" I tried to steer the conversation back to the matter at hand.

"Oh, don't worry. They'll take care of everything. You just sit tight. They'll be there in a jiffy. If you need anything else, give me a holler," Dottie said before finally hanging up.

While we waited, Vance put Rocky inside the house, and the rest of us kept our distance from the crime scene.

"Tell me it's a Halloween decoration," Deputy Jones said as he strolled into our backyard ten minutes later. Dr. Fitz, an aging werewolf shifter, and our town's medical examiner accompanied him.

"I wish." I was pretty sure the hand was the real deal, no matter how much I wanted to believe otherwise. Vance wrapped a comforting arm around my shoulder. I looked up at him and smiled. We'd solved plenty of cases together in the past, and we'd solve this one too.

Dr. Fitz slapped on a pair of rubber gloves and examined the bones. I looked away when he brought the hand up to his nose and sniffed it. Shifters were gifted in the sensory department. I should know. In my experience, having a keen sense of smell could sometimes be a curse.

"Rocky had it in his mouth," I supplied in case it was the gargoyle's scent the doctor picked up on.

Dr. Fitz nodded before saying, "It's the real deal, all right. We're going to have to clear all this out." The doctor motioned to the overgrown flowerbed.

I'd wanted help cleaning up the backyard, but not like this.

"Anything you need us to do?" Vance asked.

"Just a recount of what happened," Deputy Jones replied.

Vance looked at me. I took a deep breath and replayed the events. "There's not much. I was sitting on the swing with Misty when Rocky started to go crazy, digging in the flowerbed. I thought he was after a squirrel or something. I didn't see what caught his attention, but he was throwing dirt everywhere. That's when I went over to pull him back and saw the hand."

Deputy Jones listened intently, jotting down notes on a small notepad. "Do you know how long he was digging for?"

I looked over at Misty. "Not long," she supplied.

"Yeah, two to three minutes? Maybe not even. He has had free reign of the backyard, though. He might've been digging back here earlier." I hadn't paid attention.

"Is he just digging in this one spot?" Deputy Jones asked.

"I think so." Everyone looked around the yard. The thought of multiple bones being buried in the backyard made my stomach roll. Luckily, only the flowerbed seemed disturbed.

"But there is something else. I found a note yesterday behind the fridge. I can run in and get it.

We assume Harriet wrote it. It said something about keeping a secret. She wasn't sure if she could live with the guilt. She mentioned someone by the name of Lulu?"

"You found a confession?" Deputy Jones asked.

"I don't know, maybe."

The deputy made a few more notes before putting the pad and pen away. "Dr. Fitz is right. We need to clear all of this out." He gestured to the overgrown garden. "We'll have some workmen come in to remove the shrubbery. After you get the note, I'd appreciate it if you could stay by the house." The deputy gave me a pointed look. He knew darn well I wouldn't stay up by the house. I'd stuck my nose into other cases far less personal. It's how I became a deputy, after all.

Inside, I used my cell phone to photograph Harriet's note before passing it to Deputy Jones. I'd completely forgotten about the pizza until the delivery kid knocked on the door.

I opened the door to find the kid looking uneasy. "Sorry, this fell off," he said, handing me the door knocker.

"Oh, sorry about that." I placed the metal hardware on the floor behind me, adding it to the mental list of things to fix. When I stood, the kid looked over my shoulder into the house.

I offered him a small smile and said, "Sorry

about all the cars. It's been a crazy day. How much do I owe you?"

He shuffled his feet and said, "It's twenty-eight dollars, ma'am."

I handed him two twenty-dollar bills, and he fumbled with the change for a moment before handing it over to me. "Thanks," he said quickly, avoiding eye contact.

He turned to leave before I could even count out some change back for a tip. "Hang on."

The kid jumped.

"Sorry, didn't mean to scare you. I only wanted to give you a tip."

"Oh, yeah, right." The kid's eyes roamed to the medical examiner's van. He visibly swallowed. He probably thought there was a dead body in the dining room. I wanted to try explaining the situation, but there wasn't anything appropriate for me to say.

I ended up saying, "Thanks for the pizza," and giving him a ten-dollar tip. I could only hope the pizzeria would answer the next time we called.

I grabbed a couple of slices and headed back outside to where the group was gathered.

The workers had arrived, and I watched as they removed the overgrown shrubbery and started excavating where the hand had been found. While Vance talked with Deputy Jones, I focused on the site. I couldn't help but feel a sense of unease as I watched the dirt being dug up. What other secrets lay buried beneath the surface?

"We've got more!" One of the workers hollered to Deputy Jones. "Looks like you've got a whole body here," he said a bit quieter.

My stomach plummeted.

"I'm not going to even ask if you're taking the case," Misty said, joining me with her piece of pizza. "Just let me know what you need me to do."

"I will. Right now, I'm going to visit Mrs. Potts."

"Mrs. Potts?"

"She was friends with Harriet. Maybe she knows something." And she was the only lead I had.

I TRIED NOT to make it a habit of dropping in on people in the evening, but I figured today's events warranted an after-hours call. As a Simmering Sisters cooking club member, Mrs. Potts was known for her magical recipes, like her chicken noodle soup that could cure colds. Today was no exception. I knocked on the door of Mrs. Potts' home, taking in the aroma of something heavenly baking in the kitchen. The door opened, and Mrs. Potts greeted me with a warm smile.

"Angelica, is that you?" she said, her voice cracking. "This is a surprise. Come in, come in."

I entered her cozy living room, glancing around

at the many photographs and knick-knacks filling the space. Mrs. Potts shuffled past me and into the kitchen, where trays of cookies and other baked goods were cooling on the counter.

"I hope you don't mind me dropping by like this," I said as I followed her into the kitchen.

"Not at all, dear. It's always good to see you." Mrs. Potts seemed a little off tonight; her movements were slow and deliberate, and her words slightly slurred. She cleared her throat. "Can I get you something to drink? Tea?"

"No, I'm okay, but what about you? Are you feeling okay?"

Mrs. Potts walked over to the stove, lifted the kettle, and poured the steaming water into her teapot. "Me? Oh, I'm fine. Just feeling my age." Mrs. Potts brought the teapot to the kitchen table and joined me. "What can I do for you?"

"I'm wondering if I could ask you a couple of questions. Something's come up at the new house."

Mrs. Potts frowned. "New house? I thought you and Thelma lived at the inn?" I opened my mouth to remind Mrs. Potts that Vance and I had lived at his apartment since the wedding. "Hold that thought. My brownies need to come out." Mrs. Potts walked back to the oven and peered inside. "Well, phooey, that's not right either." The older woman sighed. "I tell you what, nothing is turning out tonight." She motioned to the trays of cooling cookies.

"I don't know. They all smell good." I eyed the assortment.

"Those are supposed to make you happy. Those are supposed to give you energy, and these, well, I can't even remember what they're supposed to do." She pointed right down the line. "All they've managed to do is make me depressed and sleepy. I don't know what's wrong with me. Maybe I'm getting too old to be baking."

"Don't say that. Let me help you." I tried to erase my concerned expression.

"Oh, don't worry about me. I'll survive. What were you here for again?"

"I wanted to talk to you about Harriet Moonstone. I understand you were friends?"

"Oh, Harriet. She's such a lovely lady. How's she doing? It's been ages since we last chatted," Mrs. Potts smiled expectantly.

"Oh, um." I fumbled over my words. I was expecting Mrs. Potts to know her friend had passed away. I took a second to find the right words. "I'm sorry. I thought you knew. Harriet passed away a couple of months back. Vance and I just bought her house."

Mrs. Potts placed a hand on her forehead, rubbing it gently. "That's right. She did, didn't she."

"Are you sure you're okay?" I reached out across the table.

"Oh, yes, dear. Just a slip of the mind. I'm fine. Go on."

I felt a pang of sympathy but pressed on. "I was wondering what Harriet was like. Did she have a lot of friends?"

Mrs. Potts thought for a moment, tapping her finger against her chin. "Well, we used to have tea together every Tuesday, and we played cards at the senior center too. She always talked about her garden. She loved it so much and her cat, Tommy. She doted on him like he was her child. Are you sure you don't want a cup?"

"Perhaps a small one."

Mrs. Potts poured us each a cup of tea.

"Did she ever mention someone by the name of Lulu?" I continued.

Mrs. Potts shook her head. "I don't know any Lulu. Harriet was a private person, you know. She didn't talk much about her family, and she didn't like to share her problems with anyone. Although, her husband Gerald had a temper. If he didn't like you, he let you know it."

"You knew Gerald?" I blew across the rim of my cup and took a sip. The hot liquid immediately brought comfort and warmth. The subtle floral notes hinted at a delicate blend, perhaps a chamomile or jasmine tea.

Mrs. Potts' eyes lit up. "Oh, yes. He was quite the charmer when he was young. He had a booming laugh that could light up a room, but when he was in a mood, watch out."

"Do you know if he had any enemies?"

"What's this about exactly?"

I took a deep breath in through my nose before answering.

"We found a skeleton buried in the backyard. I can't say for sure, but it's probably been there for a few years, at least. I'm trying to find out if Harriet knew anything about it, or maybe Gerald was responsible?"

Mrs. Potts looked shocked. "Goodness gracious! A skeleton? I would never have guessed. No, I don't know anything about that. As for Gerald, well, it's hard to say. He had a reputation, that's for sure. I could see him burying someone in the backyard if they crossed him."

"You could?"

"Absolutely." Mrs. Potts nodded, adding weight to her words.

"Do you know where he worked?"

"Oh, he was retired for thirty-plus years by the time he passed. Doubt it's someone from work."

"Unless the body's from that long ago." I thought aloud.

Mrs. Potts pursed her lips. "I suppose that's true."

"Although, I guess I could wait and see what Dr. Fitz says before digging too far into Gerald's past."

"That's not a bad idea," Mrs. Potts went to pour more tea into her cup before realizing it was still almost full.

"Can you think of anything else that might help me out? Anyone who Gerald didn't get along with?"

"That would be a pretty long list." Mrs. Potts acknowledged before taking a sip of tea. "No one specific comes to mind, but I'll think about it."

"Thank you. I'd appreciate it."

She smiled weakly. "I'm sorry, I don't know much."

"No, that's okay. You've been a big help. If you think of anything, can you give me a call?"

"Absolutely." As I stood to leave, Mrs. Potts added, "Promise me you'll be careful. You never know what you might discover in those old houses."

A lesson I was learning the hard way. "I will," I promised.

"Dorothy, you here?" a woman's voice called from the living room. I hadn't even heard her enter.

Mrs. Potts turned and called back, "In the kitchen."

A woman of a similar age to Mrs. Potts entered the kitchen. Her white hair was pulled back into a braid. She wore a jean jacket over capris and a tank top.

"Oh, sorry. I didn't know you had company."

"It's okay. I was just leaving."

"Angelica, this is Elle Raven. She took over running the art gallery when Bev moved to Florida last month."

"Nice to meet you." Elle greeted me with a warm smile, and we exchanged pleasantries.

"I'll see myself out. Enjoy your evening." I waved goodbye.

Out of the corner of my eye, I saw Elle pull a recipe book out of her bag. "I tried baking one of those delightful desserts, and it didn't turn out. Can you help?"

"Help you? Do you see my kitchen?" Mrs. Potts replied.

"Don't tell me yours didn't turn out either. I was counting on you to be the expert!" Elle said with a laugh. The two women burst into giggles. I had a feeling that together, they'd be just fine.

____

Chapter 5

____

A sense of calm washed over me when I walked into Mystic Inn. It was my family's business, and I had grown up here. It was my sanctuary. The lobby was decorated with warm colors and cozy furnishings. To the right was the registration desk, where guests could check in and out of their rooms. The white granite countertop gleamed under the light. To the left was the living room with a large stone fireplace and a flat-screen television hanging above it. Guests often gathered here in the evenings to relax and unwind. Straight ahead were glass doors that led out to the patio with the beach and lake beyond that. It was a breathtaking view and one of the reasons guests kept coming back. If you walked past the check-in desk, you'd see a set of stairs at the end and an elevator next to them. I smiled at the thought of all the memories made here over the years and headed to my office to get to work.

"What's this? You found another dead body?" Aunt Thelma asked. She was sitting behind the desk, waiting for me to walk in. She wasn't even pretending to work.

"Rocky technically found it."

My aunt gave me a level stare. It was the same look I gave her from time to time. Now I knew where I got it from.

I took a few minutes and gave Aunt Thelma the rundown of the previous afternoon. "I'm trying to look into Harriet more, given the note we found, but I'm unsure who to ask other than Mrs. Potts. Any ideas?"

"You think she's responsible for the body?" My aunt's eyes were wide.

Her expression had me second-guessing my assumptions. "I don't know. I mean, I didn't know her, but that note *was* suspicious, and the body was found in her garden." I put my purse in the bottom desk drawer and followed my aunt out front.

"I suppose that's true, but Harriet was a kind woman. I can't see her murdering someone."

Just then, Clemmie came bustling into the inn. "You found Sarah Vanhaven?" she announced. It was a good thing the lobby was empty. Clemmie was bouncing with excitement.

Aunt Thelma gasped. "My word, you're right. I can't believe I didn't think of that!"

"Who?" I asked at the same time.

Clemmie ignored me. "Mm-hmm. Who knew she was buried right next door this whole time?"

"Can you believe it? I wonder if Starry Evans will cover the story," my aunt said, referring to Witch News Network's lead reporter, who came to town from time to time. In my opinion, it was never a good day when Starry rolled into town.

But I was getting ahead of myself. I had no idea who Sarah Van-What's-Her-Name even was.

"Wait, back up. What are you guys talking about?"

"You don't know?" Clemmie looked shocked.

"Know what?" I asked.

"The Vanhavens. Jeremy and Sarah," Aunt Thelma supplied.

"I have no idea who or what you're talking about," I confessed.

"It must've all happened when she was in Chicago," Clemmie said to my aunt.

"You must be right," Aunt Thelma replied.

I looked at the two, waiting for them to get on with it.

"Jeremy's a wealthy businessman." My aunt rubbed her fingers together in the universal money sign.

"And Sarah was a successful author," Clemmie added.

"But their marriage was not a happy one."

"It certainly wasn't. Rumors swirled about infidelity," Clemmie raised her eyebrows.

"Then, one day, Sarah flat-out disappeared. POOF! Jeremy told anyone who asked that she had left town, but no one saw her go."

"Her friends and family never heard from her again."

"Does she have a family in town?" I asked.

"Oh, not anymore. I think it all became too much for them," Aunt Thelma said with a sad expression.

"You see, for a while, we all thought Jeremy killed her, but a body never turned up," Clemmie explained.

"There was zero evidence," my aunt agreed.

"Eventually, the case went cold, and people moved on but not anymore, not since you found her body."

"We don't know that," I said.

"I'd bet money on it," Clemmie wagered.

"And where's this Jeremy Vanhaven at now?" I asked.

"Why, he's your next-door neighbor!" Aunt Thelma exclaimed.

Clemmie nodded, the excitement back in her eyes. "He keeps to himself, but he still lives there, alright. I saw him looking out the window when we were helping you move in two days ago. I think we need to pay him a visit."

"I think you're right." I couldn't believe there was a potential connection between the buried body and my new neighbor. It was hard to imagine someone getting away with murder for so many years, but stranger things had happened. If it were true, I wondered what caused Jeremy and Sarah's relationship to come to such a terrible end.

There was only one way to find out.

As much as I wanted to leave Mystic Inn right that minute, I had to work. Aunt Thelma, Percy the Poltergeist, and the rest of the inn's staff were great at picking up my shifts, but I hated asking them to all the time. Besides, I wanted Vance to go with me next door, and he was currently helping the plumber check the rest of the pipes. But I called him, and Vance agreed we should interview Jeremy together. We decided to walk over after I got home later that evening.

My mind drifted to Jeremy Vanhaven's house. I'd passed by it a dozen times this week without a second thought. But that changed now that I knew the story behind the couple. The house was a simple two-story structure with faded yellow paint. It was the type of house you would flat-out ignore except for the fact that a potential killer lived inside. It gave me an eerie feeling. It was one thing to interview a random murder suspect. It was another thing when they were also your neighbor.

"Do you want to get a bite to eat first or head right over?" Vance asked when I met him at the house later that afternoon.

"Let's head over. I don't think I'll be able to eat until we talk with him."

As we approached the house, unease slid through my belly. The house was well-maintained, but the closed blinds and lack of any decor on the exterior made it look uninhabited.

Vance rang the doorbell, and we waited for what felt like an eternity before the door creaked open. Jeremy Vanhaven stood in front of us. His hair was disheveled, and there were dark circles under his eyes.

"What can I do for you?" he asked after yawning.

"Sorry, we didn't mean to wake you," I said.

"That's okay." Jeremy rubbed his left eye with his closed fist.

"We're your new neighbors. I'm Vance, and this is my wife, Angelica."

"Hello, it's nice to meet you," I added. Jeremy didn't reply. He seemed to be waiting for us to get to the point. I pressed on. "I'm not sure if you saw, but we had a bit of excitement yesterday."

Jeremy's expression remained fixed.

"Our gargoyle dug up a dead body," Vance said.

Jeremy coughed in surprise.

"I know. We were shocked, too," I said.

"We also understand that your wife went missing some time ago?" Vance asked.

Jeremy's demeanor instantly changed. "What are you implying?"

"Only wondering if you've heard from her lately." Vance kept his voice even.

"Who are you, the police?" Jeremy scoffed and went to shut the door.

I spoke up before he could. "Technically, I'm a deputy, so yes."

Jeremy stopped mid-motion and glared at me. "Get on with it then."

"I was only wondering if you ever suspected foul play?" I asked.

"No, why would I?" Jeremy folded his arms defensively across his chest.

"You never reported her missing or anything?" Vance pressed.

"I figured she'd turn up eventually. We had problems, alright?" Jeremy ran a hand through his hair.

"How long has it been since you've seen her?" I asked.

"Five years," he replied, his voice flat.

"All that time, you didn't wonder if—" I started to say.

"We're done here," Jeremy snapped, his tone

becoming hostile. "You want to talk with me? Call my lawyer. Until then, get off my property." With that, he slammed the door in our faces.

"Well then," I replied to the wood door.

"Looks like we touched a nerve."

"Yeah, I guess so."

Vance and I waited until we were safely back in our house before discussing the case.

"What do you think?" Vance asked.

"I think he has issues. He's definitely suspicious, and his claims of not suspecting foul play don't add up. Did you see how he glared at me when I mentioned my role as a deputy?"

"Yeah, he doesn't care for the police."

"Right? We should check with the sheriff and see what that's all about."

We were silent for a moment. Each lost in our thoughts.

I spoke up first. "What I can't understand is, let's say it is Sarah Vanhaven's body we found; what does that have to do with Harriet?"

"Could she have known Jeremy killed her?" Vance asked.

"And what? Let him bury Sarah in her flower bed?" It didn't make sense.

Vance rubbed his chin, lost in thought. "Maybe Jeremy paid Harriet to keep quiet. Didn't you say he had a bit of money?"

"That's what my aunt and Clemmie said." I'd

told Vance how Jeremy was a successful business-man, or he had been at one point.

I gave Vance's theory some thought. "I suppose it's possible, but I can't shake the feeling we're missing a piece of the puzzle."

"We'll just have to keep digging," Vance said with determination.

I hoped he meant it figuratively. I didn't want to find any more bones in our backyard.

After our eventful interview with our new neighbor, Vance and I decided to keep our original evening plans to get Chinese takeout for dinner and then prep the living room for paint. I realized Vance had ordered a ton of food when the delivery man offered to carry the box inside. The house was mostly empty as we weren't planning on moving in until the weekend, but the dining room table was nearby.

"Thanks, I appreciate it," I said to the nice man as he dropped the box on the table. I began taking out the containers and peering inside. We had gotten General Tso's chicken, sweet and sour pork, hot and sour soup, shrimp fried rice, and egg rolls. The smell of the food wafted through the air, making my stomach grumble in anticipation.

After we were done eating, Vance brought up the case again. "Even though Jeremy never reported Sarah missing, I wonder if there's still a file?"

"Like a cold case?" I wondered.

"Exactly."

"That's a good idea. Maybe we can start there tomorrow?" I wiped my mouth with a napkin and stood up, eager to get started with the living room.

"It's a date." Vance stood up and joined me.

We spent the rest of the night prepping the living room, moving boxes out of the way, and taping off the baseboards and windowsills. We were exhausted by the time we were finished, but the room was ready to be painted.

Chapter 6

I didn't have to work until early afternoon the next day, but Vance had to be to court bright and early. That was fine by me. Last night I couldn't sleep. I stayed awake thinking about Harriet and the note. The Moonstones had left plenty of possessions behind. Was it possible Harriet had kept a journal? And if so, could it still be in the house?

After the flood, we'd carried several boxes upstairs, and I remembered seeing notebooks in one of them. I wanted to head to the house first thing to sift through the boxes and see what I could find. I only had two hours, tops. After Vance got out of court, we would meet at the sheriff's department to ask about the cold cases before I had to work.

Seeing as our coffee pot was already packed, I stopped by La Luna on my way to the house.

Diane's bakery was cozy with a bright and

cheerful atmosphere. The large windows allowed plenty of natural light, giving the space a warm and inviting feel. The walls were painted a soft peach color, and vintage-inspired light fixtures hung from the ceiling. The delicious scent of freshly baked pastries and bread filled the air, mixed with the aroma of brewing coffee. The display case was full of beautifully decorated cakes, pies, and cookies, all tempting me. Diane was behind the counter, taking orders from the steady stream of customers. What I loved about La Luna was that it could be cold and dreary outside, yet the bakery still felt bright and warm.

"Any news?" Diane kept her voice low as she handed over my latte.

"We have more questions than answers at this point," I confessed.

"That's unfortunate."

"Tell me about it." I took a sip of my drink and went to step aside so Diane could help the next customer.

"Oh, before you go, Vance told Roger you're painting tonight. Want some help?"

"Yeah, sure. That would be great." Painting was always more fun when you had friends to help.

"Say six o'clock? I thought I could bring over a lasagna."

We planned to reheat the Chinese food, but a home-cooked meal sounded divine. That was the problem with moving. Our kitchen was packed up, and we were left eating a lot of takeout. "You're an angel," I said to my friend. "I'll pick up a salad and some wine," I added.

"Okay, see you tonight."

I waved goodbye to Diane and headed to the house.

The two-car garage was cluttered with boxes from the basement and previous ones left inside. Most of Gerald's tools were also left behind. They were haphazardly arranged on the shelves, some with rust and others looking like they had not been touched in years. The boxes were stacked high, nearly to the ceiling, and covered in dust. Some had faded labels, while others were completely blank, making it impossible to tell what they contained. The air was musty and stale, and the light from the small window was dim, casting long shadows over the cluttered space. Clearly, the garage had not been used for its intended purpose in a long time.

Upstairs was a one-bedroom apartment, which thankfully had been cleaned out. Vance and I weren't sure what we would do with the space yet; maybe fix it up and rent it out. That was a project for another day. Right now, I'd forgotten how many boxes were in the garage until I was back looking at the mess. Part of me couldn't wait for Gayle to return to town and take it all away, while the other part wanted to search every box for a clue.

I sighed, resigned to the fact that I would have to go through all of them. I pulled a box over to me and started rifling through it. The items were of little value, old books, magazines, and trinkets that no one wanted anymore. After a while, I began to feel discouraged. What if nothing in these boxes could help me solve the mystery of Harriet and Lulu?

I was about to give up when I came across a stack of journals. They looked like they had been written over several decades. My heart leaped at the possibility of uncovering some vital information. I opened a folded lawn chair, took a sip of my now-cold latte, and settled in.

I opened the first journal and was greeted by Harriet's now familiar cursive handwriting. I flipped through the pages, trying to glean any insight I could. As I read, I felt like I was getting to know Harriet. She was a woman with deep thoughts and feelings, and she poured them out onto the pages of these journals.

My heart broke for the woman as she journaled about their inability to start a family, no matter how many potions she choked down. It soared when she talked about finding fulfillment and joy volunteering at the elementary school and, later, starting a literacy program.

After reading through the first journal, I started on the second and third. Before I knew it, I had a whole stack of journals surrounding me. The more I read, the more invested I became. It was as if Harriet spoke to me from beyond the grave, sharing her innermost thoughts and secrets.

I kept my eyes open while reading for any mention of Lulu. It was almost time for me to meet Vance when I finally found something. It was only a passing reference, but it was there: "Lulu came to visit today. We had a lovely time catching up." As I said, it wasn't much, but it was a start.

However, I wasn't sure it mattered anymore because the more I read, the harder it became to picture Harriet involved with the body in her backyard. My aunt was right; Harriet had been a kind woman.

I set the stack of journals aside. There were plenty more to go through, but they would have to wait. Right then, it was time for me to head to the Sheriff's Department.

Chapter 7

I saw Vance's car parked outside when I arrived at the sheriff's department. Walking inside, I could hear Dottie's voice from down the hallway.

"I'm telling you, Vance, the sheriff really ought to put in a new security system. That old one's been on the fritz for months now, and don't even get me started on the front doors. They need to be reinforced. You can't trust people these days. You'll tell him to see to it, won't you?" she asked.

"I can certainly ask him about it," Vance said with uncertainty. No one ordered the sheriff around.

"Thank you. I knew you were just the man to ask. I was telling Angelica just the other day how much I enjoyed your wedding. It was so beautiful.

"It was. We—"

Dottie cut him off. "I'm so sorry you found

those bones in your backyard, but I'm sure that wife of yours will solve it in no time."

"Oh, well, that's very kind—"

Dottie kept right on going. She lowered her voice, but it still carried down the hall. "Don't tell the other deputies, but she's better than all of them combined. It's no secret. Everyone knows it even if they won't admit it."

Vance couldn't get more than a word in. I smiled as I watched my husband try and comment here and there to no avail.

"Angie!" Vance said, looking up and waving me over. His whole persona appeared to relax.

"Hey," I replied as I walked over to him and greeted him with a kiss on the cheek.

"Can you find the sheriff for us?" I asked Dottie.

"Sure thing!" she said with a smile. Vance and I walked away before she got another word in.

"I don't think I ever heard her take a breath," Vance said, shaking his head.

"I know," I replied with a smile.

We waited for a few minutes before Sheriff Reynolds walked out of the back room. He was a tall man in his early sixties with a no-nonsense demeanor. "Vance, Angelica, what can I do for you?"

I got right to the point. "I was hoping to talk to

you about the remains found in our backyard. Vance and I have been working the case."

"Not surprised. What have you discovered?"

I filled him in on everything, making sure he knew about the note behind the fridge and our interview with Jeremy Vanhaven. The sheriff listened intently.

When I finished, Vance asked, "Was there ever a file open on the Vanhavens?"

"Or a cold case file on Sara's disappearance?" I asked.

The sheriff shook his head. "Not that I know, but you can check downstairs."

"Downstairs?" I didn't even know there was one.

"The old records room. It's in the basement," the sheriff explained.

"You're in for a treat," Vance remarked.

"You've been down there?" I asked.

"A few times for court cases."

The sheriff led us down a narrow staircase and through a cramped hallway to a door marked 'Cold Case Files.' He opened the door, and the musty smell of old paper wafted out. "Try and solve only one cold case at a time, alright?" The sheriff motioned for us to start looking, then left the room, closing the door behind him.

The room was small and dimly lit, with shelves of boxes stretching up to the ceiling. There was barely enough room to walk between them. Some boxes had labels indicating they were from the 1970s or 1980s. Others dated further back.

Vance and I each picked a section of the room to start searching. I pulled a box off the shelf and rifled through the contents, looking for anything related to the Vanhavens or a missing person from the area. The files were in no particular order, and it was slow going.

Vance laughed.

"What? What did you find?"

"In 2002, some witch went around cursing every mailbox on Elm Street to sing Broadway tunes whenever it was opened," Vance said with a chuckle.

I grinned. "That's ridiculous."

"I know. They caught the culprit, but it's still unsolved how she did it. Some kind of singing charm."

I shook my head in disbelief. "Well, here's one for you. In 1997, a group of tourists claimed they saw a unicorn in the woods near Silverlake. The sheriff's office investigated, but they never found anything."

Vance raised an eyebrow. "A unicorn? You're kidding, right?"

I shrugged. "That's what the report says. Take a look."

I passed the file to Vance, who flipped through it

with a grin. "I had no idea our town had such interesting cases."

"I know. Maybe we should start our own investigation team."

"Now there's an idea."

Unfortunately, our enthusiasm quickly waned. After hours of searching, Vance let out a frustrated sigh. "This is a waste of time. We're never going to find anything in here."

I didn't want to give up just yet. But Vance was right; it was slow going, and as the minutes ticked by, we were running out of time before I had to head to work.

"Is there a spell we could try?" I suggested.

"I should've thought of that."

"Don't beat yourself up. We've been under a bit of pressure." We got the estimate from the plumber and the HVAC guy, and let's just say there were more zeros than either of us expected. Unfortunately, the only summoning charm I knew was Éla edó, and for that one to work, you had to picture the object you wanted clearly in your mind. Seeing as we didn't know what file we were looking for, that one wouldn't work.

Vance let out a sigh. "Yeah, that's true, but I'm not sure what spell to use."

"Me either. Let's call my aunt." She seemed to know a million different spells off the top of her head. I pulled out my cell phone only to see I had zero reception.

I practically growled. In hindsight, it was an overreaction. I could've marched back upstairs to place the call, but at that moment, I was frustrated and ready for some answers. It was ridiculous.

I reminded myself that I was a powerful witch in control of her powers. I didn't need to call my aunt.

I took out my wand and closed my eyes, focusing on the task at hand. *Find the answers*, I thought to myself. *You can do this.*

A sense of calm washed over me. I felt the familiar hum of magic coursing through my veins. I took a deep breath, and on the exhale, the words flowed easily from my lips. "Ela se ména."

As I spoke, I felt the air around me shift and change. Files began to lift off the shelves; boxes opened as the magic looked for the answer we sought. The room was filled with soft, pulsing light, and I could feel the energy building. Papers began to swirl around us. The light grew brighter. Vance grabbed the table, and I closed my eyes, focusing on the spell. It was an intense feeling, like being caught up in a whirlwind of power and possibility.

And then, as suddenly as it had started, it was over. The light vanished, and the papers settled back down onto the shelves, but there was something new on the table before us.

It was a file.

A thin, manila envelope with the name 'Morgan' written in bold letters.

I hesitated for a moment. My heart pounded in my chest. This was it, the moment we had been waiting for. Vance must have sensed my hesitation because he reached out and squeezed my hand.

"Are you ready?" he asked.

I took a deep breath and nodded. Together, we opened the file and began to read the summary.

In July 1992, a young woman named Luella Morgan disappeared from Silverlake under suspicious circumstances. She was a recent transplant to the town, having moved from Atlanta to start a new life. She worked several odd jobs, including as the receptionist at Silverlake Legal. Luella was described by those who knew her as friendly and well-liked. Despite being relatively new to the town, she had already made a few close friends, who reported her missing when she failed to show up for work one day.

The initial investigation into Luella's disappearance was intense, with police searching the town and surrounding area for any signs of the missing woman. However, as time passed and no leads emerged, the case grew cold, and the authorities eventually declared her a missing person.

"Huh." I started paging through the documents. There was a lot of information here.

"Does this mean Luella is the woman buried in our backyard?" Vance asked.

"I don't know, but we're going to find out."

Vance and I headed upstairs to the sheriff's office. As soon as we walked in, Sheriff Reynolds sat up in his chair and gave us a nod.

"What did you find?"

"It's interesting. We found a missing person's case from 1992. A woman named Luella Morgan disappeared. Do you remember the case?"

The sheriff got a far-off look in his eyes. "Now that you mention it, I do. A new girl in town. She worked for Boyd, right?"

The attorney had since retired, but he had been the founding member of Silverlake legal.

"That's the one."

The sheriff took the file from my hands and read through it to refresh his memory. "That's right. We had a few suspects early on, including Luella's ex-husband. He had a history of domestic violence, but no one ever saw him in town. We also questioned a couple of men she had dated, but we never found any hard evidence linking anyone to her disappearance."

"Do you have any idea who the lead investigator was?" Vance asked.

The sheriff furrowed his brow. "I believe it was Deputy Bishop. He was a good man. It's a shame he's since passed away."

I nodded. The Morgan file was thick. Vance and I had only skimmed the summary. I was sure there were more names to follow up with. Plus, we needed to talk with Dr. Fitz and see how we could test the remains as a match. I assumed we'd need some sort of DNA sample. "Is Dr. Fitz around?" I asked the sheriff.

He looked at the clock above his head. "No, but I'm meeting him at the top of the hour for his preliminary report."

"Mind if we join you?" I honestly wasn't sure how the sheriff would reply. Working together was still new territory. Part of me was always afraid he'd return to snapping at me.

"I suppose that would be all right. Let me grab my coat."

Fifteen minutes later, we pulled into the doctor's office.

It had been over a year since I had been in Dr. Fitz's office, and yet it looked the same as it had before. The last time Dr. Fitz redecorated his office was around the same time Luella had gone missing. His desk was light oak with a matching table along the back wall. The table was stacked with medical textbooks, framed photos, and a dusty gold nameplate.

A brown leather chair sat in front of the desk with two smaller chairs arranged in front of it, one on either side. The walls were a dull white, and the only decorations were medical diplomas and certificates. The air in the office was a mix of antiseptic and stale coffee, giving it a distinct clinical scent. The only light source came from a small window behind Dr. Fitz's desk, which looked out onto the parking lot. The blinds were half-closed, casting the room in a dim, muted light.

"Angelica, Vance," Dr. Fitz greeted us, "I'd say I'm surprised to see you, but I'm not. I knew you'd take up the case as soon as you found those bones in your backyard. Afternoon, Sheriff." The doctor turned and greeted Sheriff Reynolds.

"What've you found out, Doc?" the sheriff asked as Dr. Fitz sat behind his desk.

"I wish I had more to tell you. We know the bones belong to an adult female. The age range is broad, somewhere between twenty-five and fifty. Bone density tends to stay stable with equal amounts of bone formation and bone breakdown during those years, which aligns with our Jane Doe."

"Do you know the cause of death?" Vance asked.

"She had a cracked skull," Dr. Fitz stated, pointing to the back of his head.

"Blunt force trauma then," Sheriff Reynolds summarized.

"That's my official ruling, but as to when that happened, I'm not sure. That will take longer, and frankly, it's outside my expertise."

"What about this? We found a cold case file for a missing woman, Luella Morgan. She disappeared from Silverlake in the early nineties. Is there a way to see if she's a match?" I asked.

Dr. Fitz nodded. "Dental records and DNA would be our best bets. Do we have either of those?"

I looked at the sheriff to answer. "There was never a crime scene, so we don't have any DNA. Not sure if she was a patient of Dr. Sparrow, but we could look there for dental records." Dr. Sparrow's office was the primary dentist in the area.

"You can also look into family members. See if she ever did turn up. If not, maybe they'd be willing to submit a DNA sample," Dr. Fitz suggested.

"I can work on that," Vance offered. I agreed. Vance was better with the research, but I was happy to assist.

"You two do that. I'll see about getting a court order for the dental records," Sheriff Reynolds decided.

"Okay, it sounds like a plan," I replied. Now, if only I didn't have to hightail it to work.

Chapter 8

As I stepped into the lobby of the Mystic Inn, I noticed Percy, the inn's resident poltergeist, behind the registration desk, dealing with a trio of mortals. By the looks of it, they were all in their early twenties. Percy was checking them in, and they were glowing, which was how the residents of Silverlake knew not to do magic in front of them. To a mortal, Percy looked like an average and very much alive person.

"How'd you hear about our little town?" Percy asked the guy checking in for the group.

"Bryce's friend invited us. She owns some mansion in town. Bryce says it has a weird vibe." The guy motioned over his shoulder to his friends. The other two individuals were another guy and a girl.

"Weird vibe?" Percy questioned.

The guy leaned in closer. "Ghosts," he said with a knowing air.

Percy nodded. "I see."

"But, who knows if they're real. Those two are convinced." The man rolled his eyes. "Excuse me," he said, stepping away for a minute. The group started pulling gear out. The girl clicked her flashlight off and on several times, testing it out. The second guy had a handheld device resembling a chunky remote control.

I cocked my head, trying to figure out what they were up to, when I heard Percy mumble, "Not sure if they're real, huh?"

"Whoa! Did you see that?" Bryce exclaimed, dropping her backpack. "Scott, come here! That pen just rolled right off the table." Bryce ran over to the coffee table and knelt to check if the furniture was level. Scott, who turned out to be the one checking in, joined her.

"I'm sure the table's just not level." Scott also got down on one knee to examine the angle.

In the next moment, a stack of brochures blew off the table. "Wait, did you see that?" Bryce stood up and ran back over to the table. "Quick, Kyle. Get a reading."

I caught the poltergeist's eye and slowly shook my head. Percy had been around the inn for as long as I could remember. He had always been mischievous, but he was usually harmless. Marrying

Eleanor had mellowed him out, but I still didn't recommend antagonizing him.

"What? Didn't you hear? They're hunting ghosties. Don't want to disappoint them now, do we?" Percy whispered with a glint in his eye.

"Ghost hunters?" I whispered back, watching the group walk around the lobby, seeming to look for the unexplainable.

"Do you think Craddock House is just as haunted?" Bryce asked the guys.

"Man, I hope so! This is going to be epic," Kyle replied.

"Craddock House?" I whispered to Percy. "Mr. Craddock never crossed over?" The older man had been murdered the following summer. We solved that case, but I'd never heard anything about his ghost roaming the halls, and his granddaughter, Gabby, who lived there now, never mentioned it.

"Not the old man. There's a lady ghost who haunts the property. Eleanor doesn't even know her name, and she knows everyone. That Craddock ghost is tricky." Percy rocked back on his heels.

"Huh." I suppose I shouldn't be surprised. The Craddocks were one of the original founding families of Silverlake. A Craddock had lived at the estate for over two hundred years. It wouldn't surprise me if one of their ancestors were still kicking around the place.

Bryce approached us. "Have you ever experienced any paranormal activity in this inn?"

Percy was grinning ear to ear as he handed her their room keys. "Oh, a time or two. You never know what will go bump in the night here."

"Really?" The young woman's eyes lit up.

Percy nodded solemnly.

"Bryce, you've got to see this. The EMF readings in this room are off the charts!" Kyle exclaimed, looking down at a gadget in his hands.

Bryce raced over to join her friends. The trio began to talk over one another, excitement in their voices as they stared at the digital display and headed for the stairs. It was then that I noticed Eleanor had joined us.

"What's that all about?" Eleanor asked, eying the mortals' retreating backs skeptically.

"Ghost hunters, my love. And they're in for a treat!" Percy clapped his hands.

I looked over at Eleanor. This was going to be a disaster.

Percy chuckled as he slowly faded before us. It was all for show. The poltergeist usually disappeared in a snap when he had someplace to be. In the next instant, pens and papers floated on the desk, followed by a spooky *Ooooo!* sound. It looked like Percy was practicing. I shook my head. The ghost hunters would be lucky if they made it through the night.

It was a bit hard to focus on research while keeping one ear open for any mischief, but I managed to do a bit after getting the inn's bills paid and the housekeeping inventory ordered.

I found lots of hits on Luella Morgan. Too many. An internet search yielded over eight hundred thousand results in less than a second. This was going to take some time. At first, I quickly dismissed any obituary results, thinking I was looking for a living person, but then I realized I needed to look at those also. Thankfully, many of them had a picture I could compare with the sketch in the cold case file. No one had a photograph of Luella, but her friends had been able to describe her to the forensic artist, who completed a sketch. That, combined with Luella's birthdate, allowed me to rule out the obituaries individually. There was also an actress named Luella Morgan, but I was shocked a picture wasn't included on her IMDB profile, only her one film credit.

"Hmmm, maybe that's something," I said to the empty office.

I glanced up at the clock. It was almost time for me to leave work and head home to our painting party with Diane and Roger.

I clicked on the next page of a search and stopped to read a promising article written by *Southern Artistry Magazine*.

The headline read "Luella Morgan: The

Emerging Artist to Watch." The article was written in 1987, five years before Luella from Silverlake's disappearance.

The writer praised Luella's unique artistic style, a mix of modern and traditional techniques that was catching the attention of art lovers and collectors.

In the interview, Luella talked about her passion for art and how excited she was for her work to be recognized. She spoke of her love for the natural world and how she incorporated elements of it into her pieces.

"I want my art to inspire people and to make them see the beauty in the world around them," she said.

Luella was described as ambitious and determined, with a bright future in the art world.

But there was no picture. I had no idea if this Luella was connected to Silverlake in any way other than the magazine's publication covered artists based in the Southern United States, and Silverlake was in Georgia. Unfortunately, fifteen other states were also included.

I printed off a copy of the article and planned to take a closer look at the cold case file later tonight and see if there was any reference to Luella being an artist. Maybe Vance got lucky and was able to track down a family member, too.

My phone rang when I was driving home. It was Diane, and I could tell something was wrong from her tone when she said my name. I replied with a concerned, "Hey, what's wrong?"

"I'm sorry. We're going to have to take a rain check for tonight," Diane sounded frustrated.

"Oh no, is everything okay?" I asked, trying to keep my eyes on the road.

"I'm short help at the bakery tonight, so I have to head back in. Joys of being the boss."

"I hear you. Is there anything I can do to help?"

"No, I think I've got it covered for now. Can we reschedule dinner for tomorrow?"

"Sure. That works for us."

"Thanks, sorry again. Talk soon."

I hung up, feeling sorry Diane had to return to work. As the manager of Mystic Inn, I'd been in her position plenty of times.

When I pulled into the new house's driveway, I noticed Vance's truck wasn't there yet. It wasn't unusual for him to run late, especially since he took a few hours today to help me through the cold case files. I texted him quickly to let him know I was home and Diane and Roger needed to reschedule. He replied that he stopped by the apartment to let Rocky out and that he'd be over shortly.

The house was still mostly empty, but it was starting to feel more like a home. I couldn't wait to see what it would look like after the boxes were gone and the furniture was in place. I pulled the food from the fridge and turned on the oven to reheat it.

I was disappointed Roger and Diane couldn't make it, but I looked forward to having dinner with Vance and discussing our progress on the case.

As I waited for the food to heat up, I wandered around the house to see how the various paint swatches looked in the evening light. The only sound was the hum of the oven and the occasional creak of the old wooden floors.

I decided to take a moment to enjoy the view. We had picked this house for its location, but I was starting to fall in love with its gardens. They would be beautiful once we cleaned them up a bit. It felt like a private sanctuary. From the kitchen, I could see the sun starting to set behind the trees, turning the sky shades of orange and pink.

CRASH!

I jumped as I heard a loud crash coming from the dining room. I quickly ran to see what had happened. When I entered the room, I noticed the crystal chandelier had fallen and smashed onto the floor. The live wire was dangling from the ceiling, dangerously exposed. It sparked and crackled. It was only a matter of time before the drywall caught fire. I'd been in a fire before and did not want to repeat the experience. My heart was racing with panic. I knew I needed to turn off the power to the chandelier, but I wasn't sure how to do it. Vance was the handy one in the relationship, and he obviously wasn't home yet.

Then I remembered the fuse box downstairs. I didn't know which one controlled the chandelier, so I would have to turn them all off and figure it out later.

As I made my way down the stairs to the basement, the musty smell hit me like a wall. The dampness of the room was overwhelming, even with the floor fans Vance had set up to dry everything out. The stale air blew around the space, but at least the fans seemed to be doing some good.

I quickly scanned the room, looking for the fuse box. It was tucked next to the old fridge. I made my way over to it, careful to make sure there were no puddles on the floor. I did not need to get electrocuted.

One by one, I flipped the switches, hearing the hum of the electricity die down as each one was turned off. Finally, I got to the last one, and the house was plunged into complete darkness.

"Hello? Angie, are you here?" Vance called from upstairs.

"I'm in the basement. Watch out for the glass in the dining room!"

I could hear Vance's footsteps on the stairs, and soon he was standing beside me. "What's going on?" he asked, looking concerned.

"The chandelier fell, and the live wire was exposed," I said, still feeling the adrenaline pumping through my veins. "I couldn't find the fuse for it, so I turned off all the power to the house."

Vance nodded. Together we made our way back upstairs to assess the damage. The dining room was a mess of broken glass and shattered crystals. Still using the light from my cell phone, Vance stood on a dining room chair to inspect the dangling wire. "Looks like you did a good job turning off the power," he said, relieved. "Let's run to the hardware store and get a couple of caps so we can turn the power back on and get this cleaned up."

"Good idea. If we hurry, dinner won't be ruined." I explained how I had been reheating the Chinese food when I had to cut the power.

We spent the next hour running to the hardware store and cleaning up the mess, carefully picking up the broken pieces and wiping down the dust and debris. Somewhere in between, we managed to eat dinner. By the time we were finished, the dining room was back to its usual tidy state, but neither of us felt like painting. We decided to head back to the apartment and tackle the painting tomorrow.

"For some reason, this whole homeownership thing isn't what I expected," I commented as Vance locked up.

"You and me both. Let's hope this is the last of the disasters," he said as we followed one another down the driveway. I took a parting shot at the house over my shoulder and prayed that it would be smooth sailing from here on out.

That night as Vance and I settled in for the evening, we finally had a minute to discuss the case.

"That chandelier scare was something else," Vance said, shaking his head as we got comfortable on the couch, "Glad you're okay. You're a regular MacGyver."

I smiled, feeling a bit embarrassed but also proud of myself for staying calm and taking charge. "Thanks. It was honestly the last thing I wanted to deal with today."

"I don't blame you." Vance nodded, leaning back on the cushions. Rocky snoozed soundly at our feet.

"I forgot to tell you I found some of Harriet's old journals in the garage this morning." I stood up and retrieved the latest volume I'd been reading and handed it over.

Vance thumbed through the slim book, his eyebrows raising as he read. "Wow, these go back to the seventies. It's like a time capsule."

"I know, and Harriet seemed like such a kind woman. She wrote a lot about her garden and her volunteer work."

Vance nodded, still flipping through the pages. "Did she mention anything about Lulu?"

"That's the thing," I said, leaning closer to Vance. "She only mentioned her once, and I have no idea who she is. Did you investigate her at all?" It was a shame her sister was in Costa Rica, or I'd given her a call.

"No, not yet." Vance thought for a moment before speaking. "Did Harriet and Gerald have any kids?"

"No, she journaled about that too. They wanted them, but it never happened."

"Hmm, I wonder if Lulu is a relative of some sort," Vance suggested. "Maybe a niece or a cousin?"

"Possibly. I haven't looked into the family tree." A fact I would soon remedy. "What about you? What did you find out?"

"I looked into Luella Morgan some more."

"Was she an artist?" I interrupted, "because I found an article in *Southern Artistry Magazine* about a Luella Morgan, who was an up-and-coming artist."

"I'm not sure, but I might have tracked down her cousin in Savannah."

"Really?"

"The sheriff originally checked in with her when Luella went missing. When I searched for her name, the same address came up that was in the report. I tried to call, but the phone number was disconnected."

"Maybe it's worth a drive up the coast." I hadn't been to Savannah in years, but it was a beautiful area.

"It might be. If anything, it would help us know if she ever saw Luella again."

"I wonder if Sheriff Reynolds had any luck with the dental records or how long that process takes?"

"You know, I have no idea."

Vance and I were silent momentarily, lost in our thoughts until I remembered something. "You know who else we should talk to?"

"Who?"

"Boyd. Who knows if he remembers anything, but Luella worked for him. Maybe something will jump out." I'd interned with the retired attorney years ago in high school when I thought I wanted to attend law school. It turned out Vance was the one who'd ended up following in Boyd's footsteps. Boyd had reached out to Vance when he was retiring to see if he was interested in the practice, but Vance enjoyed criminal law more than the civil law Boyd specialized in.

"I can take tomorrow off. What about you?" I asked.

"I'm already off. It's Saturday," Vance replied.

"You're right. It is, isn't it? This has been a weird week."

"I know."

"But seeing as we're off, do you want to visit Silver Wand in the morning?" Boyd lived at Silver Wand Retirement Community.

Vance nodded. "Yeah, depending on what we

discover, we might want to head to Savannah too. It's a hike, but what do you think?"

I calculated the drive time; it would be about five hours roundtrip. A hike, for sure, but it would be worth it if we could help confirm the identity of the remains. "I think we should."

"Okay, let's plan on it then."

____

Chapter 9

____

I thought it was still early when Vance and I headed to the retirement community, but when we walked inside, it was clear that the residents had been up and at it for some time.

We were greeted with the sound of laughter and chatter coming from the common area. As we made our way to the front desk, we passed a group of ladies huddled around a table, playing cards and sipping tea. One of them, a woman with a mischievous grin, caught my eye and winked at me.

"Good morning, welcome to Silver Wand," the receptionist greeted us cheerfully. "How can I assist you today?"

"We're here to see Boyd Andrews," I replied.

"Ah, yes. He's in the common area. Just follow the laughter," the receptionist replied with a chuckle.

The common room was spacious and airy, with comfortable armchairs and sofas arranged in conversational groupings, but the tranquil atmosphere was disrupted by the sight of ferrets running amok, knocking over magazines, and pouncing on each other, trying to run away. I jumped back at the unexpected scene. The residents hooted with laughter as they shot off spells, one right after another. Streaks of pink, blue, and yellow flew across the room. I was momentarily horrified, thinking they were shooting at real animals until a spell hit one of the ferrets, and it transformed into a staff member.

"Got you, John!" a silver-haired lady said with a smile. Sitting in the oversized chair with a knitted afghan on her lap, she looked small and innocent, but her aim was impressive.

"Nice hit, Mary," John replied, laughing as he got to his feet and jogged out of the way.

As we walked through the room, several residents greeted us warmly but kept their eyes fixed on the action. Boyd was sitting in the corner, watching the chaos with a twinkle in his eye. "Well, well, if it isn't my favorite newlyweds," he said, beckoning us over.

"What's going on here?" I asked, gesturing to the ferrets and the spells.

"It's just a bit of fun," Boyd replied. "Ferret tag helps with coordination and memory." Boyd tapped his temple with his index finger. "The staff likes to keep us sharp."

"Ferret tag," Vance said to himself as he watched Mary land another spell.

"You're on fire today!" the staff member told Mary after transforming before our eyes.

"You should see armadillo tag. Tricky to land a hit with those shells." Boyd nodded solemnly.

"I bet," I remarked because what else was I supposed to say?

"If you're here to see me, that must mean you're working a case. How can I help?" Boyd leaned forward, braced his forearms on his thighs, and folded his hands.

"We're working a cold case from the nineties. Do you remember Luella Morgan? She worked for you for a couple of months." I sat across from Boyd.

"Luella Morgan?" Boyd tested out her name.

"It would have been the summer of 1992," Vance added.

Boyd nodded while thinking. "Right, she disappeared one day. Nice woman." Boyd squinted as he recalled his memories. "She didn't work for me for long, a couple of months. She needed money, but I could only offer so many hours."

"Do you think she might've left town looking for work?" Vance asked.

"I suppose it's a possibility. Not sure why she wouldn't have said something." Boyd squinted again. "If I recall, she worked at a couple of shops in Village Square too."

"Waitressing?" I asked. Luella could've worked at the diner or tavern. Vance's mom didn't own the place thirty years ago, but some of the staff had worked there for ages.

"Oh, I don't know. Too long ago to say."

"That's okay. What about Harriet Moonstone? Do you know if she was friends with her?" Vance asked.

"Why, yes. Now that I do remember. Luella rented a room from Harriet for a time there. The Moonstones rented out the room above the garage now and again. That's why I hired Luella. Harriet vouched for her. Gerald, I could do without, but Harriet was a gem."

"That's what we've heard." I looked over at Vance. If Harriet and Luella were connected, it made it possible Luella was the body found in our backyard. Now we just needed to confirm the remains belonged to her and find out what happened.

I called Sheriff Reynolds on our way to Savannah. He didn't have a copy of the dental records or even know if they existed, but he did have a court order requesting Dr. Sparrow provide them if Luella had been a patient. Seeing as it was the weekend, it would be a few days at least before we had any answers. I told him we were tracking down a potential family member and I'd call with any updates.

As we left the interstate and made our way into Savannah, the scenery changed dramatically. The trees were taller and thicker, and the Spanish moss hung down from them like ghostly fingers. The streets were narrow and winding, with old buildings that looked like they had been there for centuries. The downtown area was bustling with people, and the sounds of the city filled the air.

I could hear the clanging of the trolley bells, the chatter of tourists, and the honking of car horns. The scent of Southern cooking wafted from the restaurants, making my mouth water. Everywhere I looked, there was something to catch my eye. Quirky shops and art galleries were interspersed with historic landmarks, and the people were just as diverse.

As we drove further into the city, the architecture became more gothic, and the area's history was palpable. It was easy to get lost in the past, imagining what life must have been like hundreds of years ago, but the modern world was never far away, with shops and cafes catering to the current generation of residents and visitors.

And, of course, there were the voodoo shops, ghost tours, and cemeteries that had become synonymous with Savannah. They were tourist attractions but also part of the fabric of the city's history and culture.

I navigated Vance toward Luella's cousin's house as we drove through the city. We went through several city squares, each more picturesque than the last. The neighborhoods were lined with centuries-old oak trees, their branches draped with Spanish moss, and the roads were made of uneven cobblestones that clattered beneath our tires. I pointed out a few historic buildings, including a beautiful church with a stunning steeple that seemed to reach the sky.

Finally, we arrived at the square where the house was located. It was a beautiful home with a charming wrought-iron fence and gaslit sconces.

I followed Vance through the gate and up the cement porch. He rang the bell. After a few moments, a woman answered the door. She was younger than I expected, with long black hair and striking blue eyes.

I took the lead. "Hello, we were wondering if Marie was home?"

The woman hesitated.

"I'm sorry. Marie passed away a few years ago," she said, a hint of sadness in her voice. "I'm her daughter, Lily. Can I help you with something?"

Vance stepped forward. "Hi, Lily. My name is Vance, and this is my wife, Angelica. We're working on a case and are trying to track down Luella

Morgan. We believe she may have been related to Marie."

Lily's expression changed, and she looked at us with surprise. "Luella? I haven't heard that name in years. She was my mother's cousin."

"Would it be okay if we came in?" I asked. "It might be easier to explain if we're all sitting down."

"I suppose so. Come on in."

As we stepped inside, I noticed the house was filled with art. The walls were covered in paintings, and sculptures were on every available surface. The house smelled of turpentine and paint. It was clear that Lily was an artist, and her home was her studio. The setting looked like the art connection I'd been looking for.

We followed Lily into the living room, which was surprisingly tidy considering the number of art supplies scattered throughout the house. A large canvas was set up on an easel, and Lily picked up a paintbrush and continued working as she spoke to us. "Sorry, I just need to finish this before it dries."

"No, that's okay. Sorry for dropping by unannounced. We tried to call, but the number in the file was disconnected."

"What file is that?" Lily asked, glancing up from her canvas.

Vance answered, "Luella's missing person's file from Silverlake."

"I haven't been to Silverlake in years. It's a

charming town. Lovely lake views. There was an inn we used to stay at. Magic Inn? No, that's not right. Enchanted Inn? No. What was it called?"

I cleared my throat. "Mystic Inn. My family owns it."

"Yes! That's it. Well, what a small world." Lily slipped her paintbrush into the mason jar full of clear liquid on the side table and joined us. "Sit, please." She motioned to the couch and sat across from us in a chair. "So, you're investigating Luella's disappearance. That was so long ago. Why now?"

"We think there might be a connection to a case we're working on," I explained. "What can you tell us about her?"

Lily shook her head. "Not much, unfortunately. Luella was an artist like me. It's where my mother said I got my gift."

"I was wondering. I read an article about an artist named Luella Morgan. I wasn't sure if it was her."

"I'm sure it was. She was very talented."

"As are you." I motioned to the surrounding artwork.

"Thank you. That's so kind."

"Do you know roughly when the last time you saw her was?" Vance asked.

"Oh, decades ago." Lily glanced up and to the right as if trying to recall a memory. "She came to visit my mom once, about thirty years ago. I wasn't more than sixteen. We lost touch after that. I heard she disappeared, but I never knew what happened."

"Did she have any other family members in the area?" I asked, wondering if we could talk with them as well.

"Her sister Louisa. They were very close, according to my mom. Her, I remember more. She used to spoil me rotten with chocolates and new paints. Things like that. We'd explore the neighborhood and then return for afternoon tea parties with fancy hats and feather boas."

"Where is she now?" Vance asked before I could. I'd hoped Lily wouldn't say deceased.

"Paris, of all places. She fell in love while on vacation and hasn't been home in twenty years."

"Did *she* ever hear from her sister again?" I asked.

"No, I don't think so. I'm sure she would've told my mom. Louisa was worried sick when Lulu disappeared. It was one of the reasons she went overseas. She needed to get away."

"Did you say Lulu?" I looked at Vance.

"That was her nickname and what my mom always called her."

"And her sister's full name?" I let my question trail off.

"It was Louisa Morgan, but her last name is now Garnier. Why?"

"They might have had a mutual friend named Harriet Moonstone. Does that name ring a bell?"

Lily twisted her lips. "Sorry, I don't think so."

"That's okay." Given what Boyd had said about Harriet and Luella knowing each other, the Lulu in Harriet's journal was most likely Luella Morgan. I mentally tucked that information away.

"And what did your mom think happened to Luella?" Vance asked.

"I don't know. She didn't talk about her much. I remember when Luella first went missing, my mom thought she'd run off somewhere to paint. She was flighty like that. But when she never returned?" Lily shrugged. "I have a painting of hers if you'd like to see it." Lily stood and motioned for us to follow her into the dining room, where a large canvas took up the wall.

Vance and I both walked over to take a closer look. The painting was a landscape of a coastal scene with a vast expanse of blue sky meeting the sea in the distance. The clouds were rendered in soft, wispy strokes, giving the scene a dreamy, ethereal quality. The waves crashed against the shore in frothy white caps, and the sand was rendered in gritty, earthy tones. The overall effect was tranquil, as if the painting were a window into another, more serene world. It was clear a lot of skill and attention to detail had gone into its creation.

"It's beautiful," I said. "Do you know when she painted it?"

Lily shook her head. "I'm not sure. My mom bought it from her when she came to visit. She was struggling a bit for money at the time. Mom bought the painting to help her out. Luella was such a talented artist."

"I see that." I looked back at the painting.

"I do remember something else. Luella was preparing for a show, her first headline exhibit, I think, in Silverlake. It was supposed to be her big break." Lily's voice trailed off.

"But then she disappeared," I surmised.

Lily nodded.

"Listen, there's a chance that some remains recently turned up in Silverlake belong to Luella. They were found on Harriet Moonstone's property. We already know she was friends with Luella, and Harriet mentioned a Lulu a time or two in her journals. Silverlake's sheriff is trying to see if we can match dental records, but would you be willing to submit a DNA sample?"

Lily blinked for a moment. "Wow, I mean, yeah. It's been a family mystery for years. I'd always hoped she'd just run away, but if she's passed? I guess it would be good to know."

"Thanks. Let me call the sheriff and see if it's something we can do now or what he wants to do."

"Okay, sure."

I excused myself to place the call. I stepped into the hallway and dialed the sheriff's number. After a brief conversation, he agreed to allow me to take a DNA sample from Lily to compare to the bones found in the garden.

"You need to conjure a DNA kit from the lab here. Give me a minute to get it ready," he said.

"Okay." I sounded more confident than I felt. I knew how to conjure; I'd just never attempted it from such a distance before.

The sheriff then walked me through how to take a DNA sample with a cheek swab. It was a quick and painless process, and he explained they would then send the sample to the lab for analysis.

"If this doesn't work, we might have to bring Lily to the lab for a more extensive sample," he explained.

I joined Vance and Lily and relayed the information.

Lily nodded, looking a bit nervous. "Whatever we have to do."

I tried to give her a reassuring smile, and then we got down to business.

Surprisingly, conjuring the kit and taking the sample went off without a hitch.

"I'll let you know as soon as we get the results," I said, sealing the evidence bag.

"Right. Let me get you my number."

I put the bag on the counter and took out my cell phone. Lily relayed the digits.

When we left Lily's house, I felt like we were finally on the right track. Even though we didn't know how the woman died, if there was a DNA match, we'd at least know who she was. But at the same time, I felt a pang of sadness for Lily and her family. Living with uncertainty for all those years must have been so hard.

As we drove back to Silverlake, Vance and I discussed our next move. We agreed that we should continue to look into Luella's life and the people around her. Maybe someone knew something that happened to her all those years ago, and they were now ready to talk.

Diane called as we were crossing the wooden bridge back into town. As soon as I saw her number, I remembered our dinner plans.

"Hey, just checking to see if we're still good for tonight?" Diane said when the lines connected.

"Shoot, I completely forgot. Vance and I spent the day driving back and forth from Savannah."

"Really? That's exciting. Everything okay?"

"Hang on." I covered the receiver while I had a quick side conversation with Vance. "Remember dinner with Diane and Roger? That was supposed to be tonight. Do you still want to have them over?"

"Yeah, sure. We still need to eat, and we probably should get started on the painting." I knew what Vance meant. We had to make headway on the house, or we'd be paying another month's rent on top of our mortgage. Neither one of us wanted to do that.

I turned my attention back to the phone. "Why don't you guys come over for dinner, and we can fill you in?" Roger and Diane were older than Vance and me. If we were lucky, Maybe they remembered Luella and could help piece the case together.

"YOU FOUND LUELLA'S COUSIN?" Diane asked after I explained how my magic had found the cold case file and why we headed to Savannah. We were trimming out the living room with brushes while Vance and Roger rolled the walls. I scooted along on my bottom along the baseboard. Diane tackled the windows. Her lasagna and a loaf of garlic bread were warming up in the oven. Vance and I had stopped by the grocery store on the way home for a premade salad and a bottle of red wine to go with it. We also swung by the apartment to let Rocky out. He happily flew off the porch and took up residence at the top of the apartment building, perching on the roof. You can take the gargoyle off the roof, but you can't take the roof out of the gargoyle, or something like that.

"It was her second cousin. Her mom, who was

listed in the cold case file, has since passed," I explained.

Diane nodded thoughtfully. "I'd completely forgotten about Luella. Peter was a little boy back then. He kept me busy. It's crazy your magic found the file."

"I know, which makes me think it is her body we found in the backyard." If not, why would my magic show me the case file?

"For the life of me, I can't remember anything about a young lady disappearing," Roger confessed as he recoated his roller with paint.

"Are you kidding me?" Diane stopped trimming out the window and looked over at her husband. "She worked for you."

Roger paused, a look of confusion on his face. "Are you sure? I don't think so."

Diane gave him a knowing look. "Yes, she did. She ran deliveries for the shop."

He shook his head. "What year was this?"

"Early nineties. She disappeared summer of 1992," I answered.

Roger thought for a minute. "Honestly, I can't remember. She must not have worked for me for too long."

"I remember she came to the bakery for work, but I didn't need any help, so I sent her to you. I'm pretty sure you hired her," Diane said.

"If you say so." Roger continued rolling the wall.

"I know it was a long time ago, but do you remember anything unusual about her?" Vance asked, stepping away from the paint tray.

Diane added, "Not really. Even my memories are vague." Diane cocked her head. "She was very pretty but kept to herself. I didn't even know where she was originally from, but you know I'll come to you if I think of anything."

"Thanks, I appreciate it," I remarked. Sooner or later, we'd solve this mystery.

Chapter 10

"Good morning, you two," Heather said with a smile as she handed us menus. We decided to stop by the diner for breakfast before heading to the house. "How's the move coming along?"

"Ugh, don't ask," I said, looking at Vance.

"At least we got some painting done last night," Vance remarked.

"That's true," I conceded.

"Well, if you want help, I'm leaving here at two."

"Okay, thanks. Some friends are already coming over, but we can use all the help we can get," Vance said. Misty, Clemmie, and Aunt Thelma were all free and willing to work at the house today. Vance received a shipping notification last night, and our new furniture was being delivered tomorrow. Ready or not, it was officially move-in time.

"I'll call when I get out. Until then, what can I get you two?"

"Let's see. How about the pancakes and a side of bacon," Vance said, flipping through the menu.

"I think I'm going to change it up and go with the eggs benedict and a cup of coffee," I said, closing the menu and handing it back to Heather.

"Thanks, mom," Vance said.

As we waited for our food, I thought about the case. I was eager to get some answers but tried to be patient. I wasn't sure how long DNA tests took to process. Hopefully, it wasn't too long.

Turned out we'd have our answer soon enough.

Just as our food arrived, my phone rang. It was Sheriff Reynolds.

"Hey, Sheriff. What did you find out?"

"You're not going to like it. I don't like it," the sheriff grumbled.

"Oh no, what is it?"

Vance raised his eyebrows at my remark.

"Luella's dental records aren't a match."

"What?" I couldn't believe what I was hearing. "Are you sure?"

"Positive. The records are not even close. Luella had extensive dental work done. Dr. Sparrow said there's no way they're the same person."

I let out a frustrated sigh. It looked like we drove to Savannah for nothing. "Well, that's just great. Now, what do we do?"

"What about the Vanhavens? Did you investigate the missing wife?"

"No, not since interviewing Jeremy." We'd turned our attention away from Sarah and focused on Luella because that's what I thought my magic wanted me to do. Why had it led me astray? "Was she a patient of Dr. Sparrow?" Maybe we could compare the remains to *her* dental records.

"Unfortunately, no," the sheriff replied. "We don't know who her dentist was, and Jeremy isn't cooperative."

"Okay. Let me think on this some more." After a few more exchanges, I hung up with Sheriff Reynolds and shared my frustrations with Vance.

"Why did my magic pull out Luella's file if the remains aren't hers?"

"Maybe you used the wrong spell?"

I shrugged. "The words felt so right."

"I don't know. Maybe you're meant to solve her case, but it's not connected to the body in our backyard."

I thought about what Vance said. "I suppose that's possible."

"Don't worry about it. We'll figure it out."

"You're right." We needed to look at all the possibilities again, even if they seemed like dead ends before.

"Let's finish our breakfast and head out." Vance

reached across the table and squeezed my hand before letting go.

The past week was starting to take a toll on me. I was ready for the case to be solved and the move to be over. I picked up my fork and took a bite of my breakfast. My appetite was nonexistent, but I knew it would be a long day. We had a ton of work to do.

BROKEN TILES on the kitchen counter greeted us at the new house.

"What happened here?" Vance asked, stepping forward to examine the damage.

"Who knows? It's like the house is falling apart." First, the door knocker came off, then the plumbing and chandelier, and now this.

Up close, it looked like tiles had popped off the wall and landed on the counter, cracking in the process. The grout was old and dry like it hadn't been touched in years.

Vance pulled out his phone and took a picture. "I don't think we'll be able to match the tile." The kitchen was recently renovated, but Vance couldn't find the tiles online.

"Hello!" Aunt Thelma and Clemmie said, walking in through the front door.

"The move-in crew are in the house!" Clemmie added enthusiastically.

"Back here!" I shouted over my shoulder.

"My goodness, what's this mess?" Aunt Thelma asked, entering the kitchen.

I turned to face her and explained what had happened with the backsplash tiles. "We're going to have to replace them, and we're not sure we'll be able to find a match."

Aunt Thelma walked over to the counter and inspected the broken tiles. "Well, you'll just have to get creative. Maybe you can find some complementary tiles to mix in with the old ones," she suggested. "Do you want me to give Frederick a call and see if he can help?"

"How is he doing?" I hadn't heard much about Aunt Thelma's boyfriend lately.

"Good. Starting next week he'll be a full-time resident of Silverlake."

"That'll be different." Aunt Thelma and Frederick had spent their time split between Silverlake and Mount Holly.

"It'll be nice," Aunt Thelma replied.

Vance snapped a few more pictures of the damage. "I think I can manage it, but thanks," he said, answering Aunt Thelma's original offer for help.

Clemmie walked around the kitchen, taking in

the chaos. "I know it's been a mess, but this house has good bones."

We all looked at Clemmie.

"Alright, so wrong choice of words, but you know what I mean. The framework is nice. That's all. It's going to be beautiful once you're all settled in."

"Now that we can agree on. Where should we get started?" Aunt Thelma asked.

I looked around the kitchen. "I was hoping to finish the drawer liners and unpack the kitchen," I stated.

Clemmie clapped her hands. "Alright, we're on it."

I showed the ladies where the liners and scissors were at.

"Hey, I'm here, Misty said, walking into the kitchen. "And I brought cookies." Misty shook the pastry box before setting it on the counter and looking at the mess of tiles. "I'm not even going to ask."

"That's probably a good idea," I confessed.

"I'm going to run to the hardware store," Vance interrupted.

"Okay." I gave my hubby a soft smile. I could tell he was frustrated, but we couldn't do anything about it.

He kissed me on the cheek. "Call me if we need anything else."

I told Vance I would and then turned my focus back to Misty.

"Where do you want me?" she asked.

"Do you mind vacuuming the upstairs closets, and then we can start unpacking?"

"Not at all."

"Okay, I'm going to check on the living room paint and touch up a few spots before the furniture arrives." It was always easier to paint an empty room.

The next hour went by relatively quickly. I ended up rerolling two walls, Misty removed all the dust bunnies from upstairs, and Aunt Thelma and Clemmie were ready to put the kitchen to rights.

"Any word on the case?" Aunt Thelma asked when Misty and I joined them in the kitchen. I was directing them where I wanted everything to go. It was a work in progress, and I'd probably change my mind a time or two before everything felt right, like which drawer housed the silverware and which one for the towels—things like that.

I sighed. "Nothing good."

Aunt Thelma looked at me curiously. "What's happened?"

"The dental records don't match Luella's," I said, disappointed. "I still want to solve her disappearance, but the body in the backyard isn't hers."

Clemmie put down the box she was carrying. "You know we'll help you in any way we can."

I smiled gratefully. "I know you guys will, and I appreciate it. Right now, seeing as we ruled out Luella, I'm wondering if the remains belong to Sarah Vanhaven."

"Who?" Misty asked.

I was glad I hadn't been the only one who didn't know about the Vanhavens. I filled her in on Jeremy and Sarah's relationship and how he had been uncooperative with the police since her disappearance.

"Sounds like a red flag to me," Misty remarked.

"I know, and he was a prime suspect until we started tracking down Luella."

"What about Sarah's dental records?" Aunt Thelma asked.

"I already asked Sheriff Reynolds that. She wasn't a patient of Dr. Sparrow, so there's no way to match it unless Jeremy tells us who her dentist was."

"DNA sample?" Clemmie asked.

"If Jeremy won't give up her dentist's name, I doubt he's going to give up her DNA," Misty replied.

"Misty's right. I'm leaving that aspect up to Sheriff Reynolds. I'm not sure if a judge can force Jeremy to cooperate."

"I've got an idea. How about Clemmie and I look into Luella more? We'll see who else was working for Boyd back then. Maybe they know something."

"Okay, I'll look into the artist angle a bit too. Her cousin said she was supposed to headline a show before she disappeared," I added.

"That gallery might know something," Misty said.

"I know. I'm going to check with Elle tomorrow. In the meantime, Vance and I will do a background check on Sarah tonight."

"Hopefully, she simply moved away," Misty said.

"I hope so too. Jeremy said they had problems."

"So, it's possible," Misty replied.

"I think so." And if that were the case, maybe she wouldn't be that hard to find.

As we continued to work on unpacking, Clemmie suddenly asked, "What time is it?"

Aunt Thelma looked at her watch. "It's almost two o'clock. Why, dear?"

Clemmie's face lit up. "Oh, I forgot I have a date tonight! I've got to go get ready."

"Another one?" I asked.

"Is it the same guy?" Misty chimed in.

"What's his name?" Aunt Thelma asked.

"Yes, another one. No, it's not the same guy, and no, I'm not telling you his name. Now if you'll excuse me, I need to get to gettin'."

"I hope she knows what she's doing," I told my aunt and Misty.

My comment must have sparked a thought as Misty stood abruptly.

"Hey! Ask him to take a picture with today's newspaper and send it to you!" she shouted after Clemmie.

"Now, why would I go and make him do that?" Clemmie leaned back inside the kitchen.

"Yeah, why would she go and do that?" Aunt Thelma asked.

Misty and I shook our heads as if the answer weren't obvious. "Because you want to make sure he's who he says he is!" I explained.

"Right. He could be some smooth-talking creep using some photo he stole off the internet," Misty said.

"And if he is, I'll curse him to next week. Mark my words!" Clemmie thrust her pointer finger into the air.

I couldn't help but laugh at her remark. "Well, let's hope it doesn't come to that."

"I'm serious. I've got some spells that would make his head spin," Clemmie said with a smirk.

"Just be careful," Misty said over Clemmie's remarks.

"Oh, I will be. Don't you worry. I'm a grown woman. I can take care of myself," Clemmie said, waving as she walked out the door.

"I hope so," I murmured as I watched her leave. Online dating could be tricky, and I couldn't help but worry about Clemmie, but I knew there was no point in trying to stop her. She would do what she wanted regardless of what we said.

Once the kitchen was fully unpacked, we moved on to the upstairs. Aunt Thelma and I worked on unpacking the master bedroom while Misty tackled the guest room. Aunt Thelma brought up the topic of the ghost hunters staying at the inn while we made the bed.

"Why didn't you tell me we had a bunch of ghost-hunting mortals staying at the inn? My word! Percy is having fun at their expense. One of the guys checked out this morning! Didn't even ask for a refund."

I tried not to laugh, but I wasn't surprised. "I forgot to mention them to you. They're supposed to be looking into a ghost who haunts Craddock House. Do you know anything about that?"

"A ghost at Craddock House? Can't say that I do."

"Percy knows of her, but even he said she was elusive."

"Well, regardless, the hunters didn't need to go far to find a ghost. Percy gave them a show complete with clanking chains and wailing at three o'clock in the morning."

"He didn't! Those poor people. They're in way over their heads." Most mortals didn't even know Silverlake existed, let alone come here and investigate. We had ghosts around every corner. Here, they were more like family.

"You got that right. I met them yesterday, and they seemed a bit inexperienced," Aunt Thelma said.

"Maybe we should offer to help them out," Misty suggested as she walked into the bedroom with an armful of linens. "I mean, we do have some experience with the paranormal."

"I don't know," Aunt Thelma said, looking skeptical. "Those hunters are mortals; we don't want to expose ourselves unnecessarily."

"True, but the sooner we get those guys out of here, the better. In fact, it would be better if they didn't encounter any ghosts at all."

Misty's eyes widened. "You don't think they'll tell their friends, do you?"

"I'd almost guarantee it." And then we'll have ghost hunters visiting from all over the world. Silverlake thrived on tourism, but it was ninety-nine percent from the supernatural community. It would get exhausting having to hide our true identities if mortals started vacationing here regularly. Silverlake was the one place where we could be ourselves.

"We can't do anything about Percy's show now," Aunt Thelma remarked, "but I'll talk to him and tell him to tone it down. Maybe we can come up with some elaborate explanation for Percy's paranormal exposition."

"Or maybe we just zap their memories," Misty said matter-of-factly.

"Or maybe we do that," Aunt Thelma agreed.

It was illegal to alter another witch's memories, but it wasn't illegal to alter mortals', especially if it was to keep our supernatural secrets safe. "We'll see if it comes to that," I added. Hopefully, we can explain the unexplainable and send the ghost hunters on their merry way. Which reminded me: I should stop by Craddock House, talk to Gabby, and find out exactly how the ghost hunters came to know about her house in the first place.

Chapter 11

That night was the first night Vance and I spent in our new home. As I looked around the partially unfurnished house, I felt a pang of homesickness for our apartment, which was silly. I had never been particularly fond of the place, but still, it had been ours. I pushed the feeling aside, determined to make this house our home. I wondered if I should ask my friend, Honor, to enchant our home like she had done for her sister. Honor's magic created a warm, cozy atmosphere that made you feel instantly at ease. It was something I could use in this new, unfamiliar space. I made a mental note to call her tomorrow to see if she could help.

Seeing as the living room was mostly furnished, I planned on pulling out a blanket and curling up on the couch with my computer to research Sarah

Vanhaven while Vance finished replacing the last fallen tile on the backsplash. I'd just found my favorite fleece blanket when we heard a loud crash from the upstairs bathroom.

"What was that?" I asked, feeling a jolt of adrenaline.

Vance didn't say anything as he quickly ascended the stairs, and I followed close behind. When we got to the bathroom, we saw one of the bathroom shelves lying on the ground, surrounded by a mess of my lotions and soaps. The second shelf hung at an angle with its screws pulled out of the drywall. The shelves had been mounted to the wall above the sink. The large mirror above the sink was still intact.

"That's weird," Vance said, removing the remaining shelf and examining the wall where it had been attached.

"Do you think it was because of the tile falling earlier? Something faulty with the adhesive?" I asked, trying to come up with a logical explanation. "Maybe Gayle did a couple of projects around the house before listing the house for sale, and things didn't hold as she'd expected?'

Vance shook his head. "I don't think so. This was attached with screws, not adhesive."

"Hmmm. It must just be a fluke," I said, trying to brush off the uneasy feeling creeping up my spine.

"I don't know. It's odd."

We looked around the bathroom, but nothing else seemed out of place. Neither of us wanted to say anything, but I knew we were thinking it—something wasn't quite right in our new home.

Needless to say, I had difficulty settling in for the night. Thankfully, I had plenty of other thoughts to occupy my mind, starting with Sarah Vanhaven.

"Do you want me to start searching the legal databases?" Vance offered from his side of the bed. We were tucked in for the night.

"Sure, why don't you do that, and I'll scour social media?"

Vance nodded and pulled out his laptop. I opened my phone and began my search. It wasn't long before I found a Facebook page for a woman who shared Sarah's last name. I clicked on it and started scrolling through her posts. Most were pictures of her kids and pets, but one post caught my eye.

"Happy birthday to my beautiful sister, Sarah. I miss you every day."

I showed Vance the birthday tribute. "If Sarah's still missing..." I let my words trail off.

"It means she didn't run back to her family," Vance finished my thought.

Which made it more likely that something terrible had happened to her.

"Looks like we have a lead," Vance said, typing the sister's name into the legal database.

I continued scrolling through the page, hoping to find more information about Sarah's disappearance, but there wasn't much to go on—only a few comments from friends expressing their sadness and longing for Sarah to come home. I made a note of the names.

Vance interrupted my scrolling. "Based on her sister's info, I found a few other family members we can follow up with. It looks like Sarah's parents are still alive and living in Ohio."

"But you found nothing on Sarah, right?"

"Right."

We continued searching for Sarah, reading through social media posts and legal databases for any trace of her. The only thing that I could find were copies of her books. They looked to be true crime novels based on the covers. The last one was published the year before she disappeared. I had never read any of her books. I tended to avoid reading true crime. I'd experienced it enough in my personal life.

After a while, we hit a dead end. There was no sign of the woman online or in any legal documents. We even tried facial recognition, allowing Google to search the internet for Sarah's picture. It was as if Sarah had vanished without a trace.

"I think we should follow up with the family in the morning," Vance suggested, stifling a yawn.

"Yeah, I guess we'll have to." Vance yawning made me yawn. I put down my phone as he closed the laptop. I thought falling asleep would take me forever, but I was blissfully in dreamland within minutes, tucked up against Vance's side.

Chapter 12

The next morning was Monday, and Vance was up early, heading into the office. He planned on contacting Sarah's family to see if they had any information on her whereabouts or when the last time was that they saw her. Depending on what they said, I was going to talk to the sheriff and see about obtaining a DNA sample to compare with the remains.

In the meantime, I decided to honor my magical hit and continue looking for Luella.

I made a mental checklist of what I wanted to accomplish that day: first, call Boyd's office and see if any other former employees worked there around the time of Luella's disappearance; second, visit the art gallery to see if they have any information on Luella or her artwork; and after that, I had to head to work.

With a quick kiss goodbye, Vance headed out the door to start his day. I sat at the kitchen table with a fresh cup of coffee and my notebook, ready to make my call.

I dialed the number to Silverlake Legal and was put on hold for a handful of minutes before a woman got back to me.

"Silverlake Legal, how can I help you?" the friendly receptionist asked.

"Hi, this is Angelica Blackwell."

"Oh, hi, Angelica, it's Cindy. How's your aunt doing?"

I had no idea who Cindy was, but everyone knew Aunt Thelma.

"She's doing well, thank you. Listen, I'm working on a cold case for Sheriff Reynolds. We're looking into the disappearance of Luella Morgan. She worked for Boyd back in the early nineties."

"Oh, well, she'd be before my time here then."

"I know, mine too, but I went and talked to Boyd yesterday. He vaguely remembered her. I was wondering, is there anyone else there who might remember her? Mrs. Jones, perhaps?" Mrs. Jones had been Boyd's paralegal for years. As far as I knew, she still worked for the new group.

"Oh, she's here all right. Hold on a moment; I'll put you through."

After a brief hold, I was transferred to Mrs.

Jones. She sounded older, but her memory seemed as sharp as ever.

"Hello, Angelica. What can I help you with?" she asked.

"I'm looking into the disappearance of Luella Morgan. She worked for Boyd back in the summer of '92. I was wondering if you remember her?"

There was a pause, and I wasn't sure if she remembered anything, but then she spoke up. "Oh, yes, I do remember her. She was a sweet girl, quiet but talented. She used to paint during her lunch hour, right in the break room. She had an easel set up and everything."

"Interesting. Did she ever mention anything about her personal life?"

"No, not really." Mrs. Jones paused momentarily before continuing, "I do remember she talked about an upcoming gallery opening. She seemed nervous about it. She said she didn't think her work was good enough."

"Did she happen to mention the name of the gallery?" I asked.

"Oh sure, it was the one right here in town."

My heart skipped a beat. I was right to follow up with the gallery next. "Thank you, Mrs. Jones. You've been very helpful."

"You're welcome, Angelica. Good luck with your case."

I WALKED INTO THE GALLERY, taking in the surroundings. The space was bright, with high ceilings that gave the gallery an airy feel. The walls were painted a soft white that complemented the artwork. Some paintings had thick, ornate frames, while others had none.

"Hi, Angelica." I turned at the mention of my name and spotted Honor at the front counter talking with Heidi. I liked Heidi. She'd moved to Silverlake some time ago when I'd been living in Chicago and had worked at the gallery ever since, even after Bev retired.

Honor had a couple of charms in the palm of her hand. They were attached to long silver chains and sparkled in the light.

"Hey, how's it going?" I asked, joining them.

"I was talking to Heidi about stocking some of my charms here. I thought maybe I could set up a small display in exchange for displaying some artwork at my shop."

"I think that's a great idea. Your charms are works of art." My hand instinctively went up to the protection charm I'd bought from Honor last winter. I wore it every day, along with my tiger's eye amulet. The amulet gave me, and only me, the power to transform into my feline alter ego, Penelope.

"I think it's a great idea too. I just need to clear it with Elle. She's in the back, packing up a few orders. Can I call you after I get a chance to talk with her? Oh, what were you thinking in terms of commission?" Heidi asked Honor. I stepped back to allow the women to talk business.

As I walked further into the gallery, I was immediately drawn to a painting hanging on the wall.

The painting depicted a village much like Village Square, the storybook-like shopping district the gallery was a part of. The artist used loose brushstrokes to capture the essence of the colorful storefronts and the bustling activity of the square. The sunlight filtered through the trees, casting dappled shadows on the cobblestone streets. The colors were bright and lively, with pinks, yellows, and blues dancing across the canvas. It was a beautiful representation of an idyllic village.

As I perused the paintings, I suddenly saw a familiar figure dusting the artwork with a soft cloth in the back corner. It was Mrs. Potts.

"Mrs. Potts," I said with surprise.

She turned to look at me, but for a moment, her expression was blank. Then recognition dawned on her face. "Angelica! Oh my, sorry. Took my mind a moment to place your face."

That was a first. I thought back to earlier last week in her kitchen. Mrs. Potts' memory problems seemed to be getting worse. I tried not to let my concern show on my face. I cleared my throat. "What are you doing here?"

"I work here now. Isn't that something?" She gestured around the gallery. "She's gotten all these new pieces in. The least I could do is get them ready for sale."

I eyed the artwork once more. Various frames were stacked along the wall; others were still wrapped, waiting to be displayed. Mrs. Potts was right. The gallery was stocked.

As I took in the paintings, Elle came waltzing by with a cardboard box and bubble wrap, looking like she was on a mission. Even though she was about the same age as Mrs. Potts, she seemed years younger. She was talking to Mrs. Potts about packaging up the next piece when she noticed me.

"It's Angelica, right? How nice to see you," Elle said, a smile spreading across her face.

"Nice to see you too. These paintings are beautiful," I replied.

"I know. We've got some great ones in," she said, gesturing to the paintings on the walls.

Elle then turned her attention back to Mrs. Potts. "Let's get this piece wrapped up and ready to go; then we'll move on to packaging the next one."

"Okay," Mrs. Potts replied, setting down her cloth and taking the packing materials from Elle.

Elle waited until Mrs. Potts was out of earshot. "I have to be honest with you. I'm worried about

Dorothy," she said in a hushed tone. "That's why I have her here at the gallery. It's easier to keep an eye on her."

My heart sank. "You don't think she can be alone?"

"I don't think so. I know we don't know each other well, but I can tell you care for her, and you've known her for years. Do you know if she has any family we could talk to?"

I thought for a moment. "She never had any children, but she has some nieces and nephews she's mentioned a time or two. I'll see what I can find out."

"That would be great. With the way her memory is going, I'm worried she won't be able to live alone for much longer."

I nodded, unable to find the right words.

Elle turned to walk away before I remembered the reason for my visit. "Wait, real quick, do you know if Bev kept any records from the nineties? I'm trying to track down some information on Luella Morgan."

Elle's face clouded with concern. "Luella Morgan? Why are you looking for her?"

"It's a long story. Basically, I stumbled upon her cold case, and now I'm trying to solve it."

"Oh, it's just…well, that's me," Elle said, her voice barely above a whisper.

"Excuse me?"

"I'm Luella Morgan, or I was." Elle suddenly looked uncomfortable. "I haven't heard that name in years. Decades, really."

I was stunned. "Wait, you're Luella Morgan?"

Elle nodded. "Yes, that's my birth name anyway. I changed it after I left Silverlake."

"But why?" I blurted out.

Elle seemed annoyed with herself. "It was foolish; imposter syndrome, I suppose. Back then, I was just starting out in the art world. I didn't think my work was good enough. I flaked on a few galleries and knew no one would give me a second chance. So, I decided to start fresh somewhere else."

I couldn't believe it. I had found Luella Morgan, or rather, Elle. I had so many questions. "Why did you leave without telling anyone?"

"I guess I panicked," Elle admitted. "I was out of money and didn't have enough paintings for the show. I felt like a failure and just ran away from it all. I know it was a stupid thing to do, but I was young."

"But you must have known that people would be looking for you. The police, your family..."

"I didn't think anyone cared. My family didn't care about me. My sister pretended to, but secretly she was jealous. I know that sounds awful, but it's true. I called her a few times in Paris, but she never took my call, and when my cousin told me she was done supporting me, I knew I was truly alone."

I felt a pang of sadness for her. "What about your friends?" I asked. "Didn't you have anyone you could turn to?"

Elle shook her head. "No, not really. I was always so focused on my art I didn't have time for anything else, and when I left Silverlake, I didn't keep in touch with anyone. I just wanted to forget about my past and start over."

"I'm sorry," I said, not knowing what else to say.

Elle shrugged. "It's in the past now, and everything worked out for the best. I've had a thriving art career, and my business is doing well. Truthfully, it's good to be back. I always loved Silverlake."

Elle smiled and turned to walk away. I stopped her. "So that you know, not everyone in your family forgot you. I know you said your cousin cut you off. I assume you mean Marie?"

"You know her?"

"No, but I met her daughter."

"Lily?" Elle's face lit up.

"Yes, and she still remembers you. She said that she always wondered what had happened. I have her number. Would you like to call her?"

Elle hesitated. She exhaled. "I don't know."

"Or would it be okay if I called her? I think she deserves to know you're alive. She submitted a DNA sample and everything to help us locate you."

"She did?" Elle seemed shocked. "I didn't think

anyone cared." The woman sighed. "I suppose that would be all right."

"Okay. I'll give you her number, too, just in case you want to talk with her yourself."

Elle nodded.

As I wrote down Lily's number for Elle, I couldn't believe the case of Luella Morgan was officially closed. I didn't think I'd actually find her today, let alone talk with her. I handed the number over. "You were friends with Harriet, too, weren't you?"

"Harriet?"

"Harriet Moonstone."

"Oh yes, sorry. Too many names are floating around in my brain. Harriet was a lovely woman. I'm ever grateful to her. She gave me a home when I didn't have one and food in my belly, too. Unfortunately, being a starving artist is all too often the reality."

"I bet." I nodded in understanding. "I was wondering how well you knew her."

"We were good friends for a short time. I was sorry to hear she'd passed. I would've liked to see her again."

"This might sound weird, but do you know anything about a note she wrote in her journal? It said *Lulu will never forgive me if I confess, but I don't know if I can live with this secret.* What was that about?"

Elle let out a laugh. "I can only imagine. Harriet

could be a bit dramatic." Elle thought for a moment. "Although, she did cheat at a baking contest once."

"Baking contest?" I cocked my head.

"I bet that's it. It was supposed to be an original recipe, but Harriet used a Betty Crocker one, thinking witches wouldn't be any wiser, and she was right! She won the five-hundred-dollar cash prize and used the money for a new oven, which she desperately needed."

"But?"

"She didn't like lying. I told her I'd never forgive her if we all starved because she had no oven to bake in." Elle shook her head.

"What did Gerald think about that."

"You've heard about him, huh?"

"A few things."

Elle's expression turned dark. "He wasn't happy. Gerald was the man of the house and thought he should provide everything, but he'd just been laid off from work and couldn't afford a new one. He had to swallow his pride. Harriet was worried about his temper. She wanted to leave him but didn't have anywhere to go. She was afraid of what he might do if she left."

I felt a pang of sadness for Harriet. It sounded like she was in a tough situation. "Did she ever confide in you about that?" I asked.

"A little, but she didn't talk about it much.

Harriet wasn't one to complain," Elle said, shaking her head. "I should've had her come with me. That's my one regret, leaving her behind."

"I don't know. You can't be responsible for other people's choices. She might not have gone with you, either.

"True, but I should've at least asked." Elle twisted her lips and looked like she might cry.

I instinctively wrapped her in a hug. "You did the best you could at the time. Remember that. It doesn't do you any good to beat yourself up over the past. Besides, it sounds like you were dealing with your own crisis."

Elle smiled. "That's true. Hindsight is twenty-twenty, as they say."

I followed Elle up to the front of the store on my way out. Honor was still chatting with Heidi.

"Oh, before I forget, would you be willing to put a relaxing charm on my new house or whatever it was you did to your sister's place that one time to make her house so calm and inviting?"

Honor looked confused for a moment before recognition dawned on her face. "Oh, sure! I can stop by tonight after work if you're good with that."

"Shoot, I have to work, but Vance will be home. Is that okay?"

"Absolutely. Tell him I'll be over by seven."

"Okay, thanks. Bye, ladies." I waved goodbye on my way out the door.

Chapter 13

When I left the art gallery, my phone buzzed in my pocket. It was Vance. I quickly answered.

"Hey, guess what?" I said before he could even speak.

"What?"

"I found Luella Morgan."

"What? Where?"

"Well, she goes by Elle now, and she's the new art gallery owner where Luella was supposed to have her show. She left town years ago without telling anyone, changed her name, and started over."

"That's incredible. You've solved one of the mysteries."

"True, and I also found out some interesting information about Gerald. Luella mentioned that Harriet was worried about his temper and wanted to leave him."

"Didn't someone else say he had a temper?"

I thought for a moment. "Mrs. Potts said something similar. Oh, and she was there too. Her memory is really going. Elle's having her work at the shop to keep an eye on her."

"What? Man, that's too bad."

"I know. I told her I'd try and track down her family. Maybe they can come up to pay a visit." I had no idea who Mrs. Potts had lined up as her caregiver or medical power of attorney, but I cared enough for my former teacher to find out.

"That's a good idea."

"How about you? How's your morning going?"

"I made a call to Sarah's parents. They said they hadn't seen or heard from their daughter in almost five years; not since Jeremy said she left town."

I frowned. "That's not a good sign."

"No, it's not."

"Did she say anything about leaving Jeremy?"

"Not to her parents. I called her sister, Alice, and left a message."

"Do you think I should talk to the sheriff about a DNA test for them?"

"I think it's the logical next step. I told them we were relooking at the cold cases in Silverlake, but I didn't mention the remains. I didn't want to upset them if I didn't have to."

"That's smart," I said, nodding in agreement.

"I'll talk to Sheriff Reynolds and see what he thinks."

"Let me know what he says," Vance replied.

We said our goodbyes and hung up. I took a deep breath and decided to call the sheriff right away. I needed to know what our next move was.

After a few rings, Sheriff Reynolds picked up. "Sheriff, it's Angelica Blackwell. I have some news about Sarah Vanhaven."

"What did you find?" he asked eagerly.

"We were able to track down her family. Vance talked to her parents and left a message with her sister, but I was wondering if we should request a DNA test from them. It might help with the identification of the remains."

There was a moment of silence on the other end. "It's worth a shot. I'll take care of it on my end."

"Thank you, Sheriff. I appreciate it," I said gratefully.

"Keep me updated if you find anything else."

"I will," I promised, hanging up the phone. It felt good to make progress on the case, even if it was just a small step forward.

When I got to work, I found Percy sulking in the back office; his arms crossed in front of his chest. Aunt Thelma had evidently scolded him for messing with the ghost hunters. I couldn't help but smile at the sight of him pouting like a child.

"Come on, Percy. You know we don't want a bunch of ghost hunters coming to Silverlake," I said, trying to reason with him.

"But it would be fun!" he protested.

I rolled my eyes. "Fun for you, maybe, but not for the rest of us."

As I walked out of the back office, I was greeted by Eleanor. "Percy, stop being ridiculous and come run some errands with me," she said, glancing over at me. "I promise I'll keep him out of your hair."

"It's okay. I'm used to it."

"See, Jelly doesn't think I'm being ridiculous," Percy said, referring to my childhood nickname.

"Oh no, you are being ridiculous. What I said was that I was *used* to it."

Percy stuck out his tongue before turning to his wife. Being forced to be good was grinding on the poltergeist's nerves.

Eleanor looked at him disapprovingly.

"Fine," Percy huffed, "but no clothes shopping."

Eleanor rolled her eyes and grabbed Percy's hand, pulling him towards the door. "We'll be back in a bit," she said with a wink.

I walked behind the registration desk and took up my post. Aunt Thelma walked down the stairs moments later.

"Was that Percy who just left?"

"Mm-hm."

"Good. He's been whining nonstop. I told him

he could go harass mortals someplace else, but he said it wasn't as much fun as it was here."

"Of course he did."

Aunt Thelma and I stopped talking abruptly as we heard the elevator ding. We turned to see the remaining ghost hunters stepping out; their attention focused on the back of their camera as if they were re-watching footage.

They were so engrossed in what they were doing that they didn't even notice us at first. It wasn't until they turned around and saw us standing there that they snapped out of their trance.

"How's the ghost hunting going?" I asked.

"It was amazing!" exclaimed Bryce. "I've never seen anything like it!"

Kyle nodded in agreement. "Yeah, it was a full apparition. I couldn't get my camera to record fast enough."

"Was this at Craddock House?"

"On the property, yeah," Bryce said.

"By the old barn," Kyle added. They were both looking at the back of the camera again.

Aunt Thelma raised an eyebrow. "And what did this apparition look like?"

"It was a woman," Bryce said excitedly. "She had long, flowing hair. She was so beautiful."

Kyle chimed in, "She was walking towards the house like she was going to go inside."

"But she didn't. She kept looking over her shoulder at us. It was sort of sad," Bryce added.

"Sad?" Aunt Thelma asked.

"I don't know. I can't explain it, but I felt sad like I was feeling her emotions or something. It was weird."

"This whole town is weird," Kyle told Bryce before turning to us. "No offense."

"None taken," I replied, imagining how weirded out the duo would be if they knew half the truth. I focused on the subject at hand. "Did you get any footage?" I asked.

"That's what we're trying to see. I don't think so," Bryce said.

"My hands were shaking so badly. I couldn't even think, but we'll keep trying," Kyle added with a determined look. "We're not leaving until we capture something."

That's exactly what I was afraid of.

AFTER WORKING the rest of the day, I decided to stop by Craddock House to talk with Gabby. Ghosts were the norm around Silverlake, so I wasn't sure what was so special about this one or why she'd invited a group of mortals to visit.

Everyone knew Craddock House, even if they were only passing through. The property had a plaque displayed out front declaring it a historical landmark.

Craddock House was an impressive structure with an imposing grandeur that commanded attention. It was a two-story Victorian mansion with a wrap-around porch and a steep, slate roof. The exterior was painted in a muted gray-green hue that complemented the verdant foliage surrounding it.

The front yard was expansive and meticulously landscaped with bushes trimmed into whimsical shapes and a flower garden stretched for acres. The lawn was so perfectly manicured that it almost seemed unreal, like it was part of a movie set, especially the backyard with its brick patio, three-tiered fountain, and hedge maze.

The mansion's interior was even grander. The walls were covered in intricate floral wallpaper, and the floors were polished hardwood. The rooms were spacious and filled with antique furniture and priceless artworks, giving the house an old-world charm. The living room was the most impressive, with a grand piano in the corner, an ornate chandelier hanging from the ceiling, and a fireplace that stretched almost the entire wall length.

When I was a little girl, Mr. Craddock used to host a summer barbeque and invite the entire town. After stuffing ourselves silly, we'd run through the hedge maze playing tag or head inside for the best game of hide and seek ever. Never once did I suspect the property was haunted when I was little, but then again, I lived with Percy. Ghosts were the norm in my life.

Gabby greeted me at the door with a warm smile. "Angelica, what brings you by?"

"Hey, do you have a second to talk? I wanted to chat about the mortals who've been ghost-hunting here. I think one is a friend of yours?"

"Bryce, yes. Sorry, I should've given you a heads up."

"No, that's okay, but I am worried about them bringing other mortals to the area."

"They're still allowed in, aren't they? The town council said they could come."

"Yes, absolutely. I just don't want word of all the paranormal activity around here to get around and have it become something bigger."

"Ooooh, I got you. I didn't think of that. It's just Bryce visited shortly after I inherited the place, and she immediately picked up on the paranormal vibe. I know she's a mortal, but she's sensitive to the supernatural, which was probably why we became fast friends in college. Anyway, I thought maybe she could help."

"Help how?"

"The ghost on the property? There's something that's not quite right about her. I'm not sure what's wrong. She's always running away and looking over her shoulder."

"Like she's scared of you?"

"I don't think so. More like she's checking to see if I'm following her."

"And do you?"

"Never. Would you?"

"Probably not." I thought for a moment. "Does she ever say anything?" Most ghosts I knew were very sociable.

"Never, which I know isn't normal. I mean, I asked the banshee at the bed and breakfast what she thought, and even she quit wailing long enough to talk to me."

I smiled. Melinda did like to wail.

"Did she have any ideas?"

"None. She said the Craddock ghost keeps to herself and likes it that way."

"Huh, and you don't know who she is?"

"Not a clue. My grandfather never mentioned her. I don't know if she's a relative or what. I didn't know anything about her until I was picking apples in the orchard and stumbled upon her."

"You don't remember seeing her when you were younger?"

"No, do you?"

"No. We used to play here every summer too."

"I remember that."

I thought for a moment. "Would it be okay if I come back with Percy or Eleanor to try and talk with her?"

Gabby nodded. "Of course. I don't see why not."

"Thanks. I just want to see if we can help her in any way."

"Sure, and I'll talk to Bryce. I'll tell her Silverlake is special, and we don't want it to become a spectacle."

"Thanks, I appreciate it. I'll call you beforehand so you know when we're here."

"Okay, that would be great. Thanks."

Chapter 14

Vance and I spent a rare, ordinary evening at home. We watched a movie, ate popcorn, and cuddled on the couch. There were no ghostly interruptions or magical mishaps to deal with. It was a much-needed break from the chaos consuming our daily lives.

As we settled in for the night, Vance turned to me with a smile. "It feels good to have a moment like this with just us, enjoying each other's company."

I nodded in agreement. "It does. I almost forgot what having a quiet evening at home was like." As promised, Honor met Vance over here after closing her shop for the night and got to work. As we sat on the couch, I felt a sense of calm wash over me. The house felt different, in a good way. The air felt lighter, and there was a warm and welcoming feeling throughout the space. It was as if the charm had infused our home with love and comfort, making it the perfect place to relax and unwind. I snuggled closer to Vance, grateful for this moment of peace and contentment.

Rocky was spending more and more time outside, which I didn't mind. I loved the gargoyle, but it was hard keeping him inside full-time. He'd spent two hundred years perched on the church's bell tower with his buddy, Ralph, and seemed more at home outside, where he could fly around at leisure.

Vance and I had been enjoying the peace of our enchanted home so much that we'd both fallen asleep on the couch.

A few hours later, I woke with a start.

"What was that?" I whispered into the darkness.

"Hmmm?" Vance mumbled, still not awake.

In the next instant, chaos erupted. Rocky began to go nuts outside. We could hear him running around and barking, knocking over the trash cans as he went. At first, I thought he was chasing after a cat or some other animal, but then we heard a window shatter.

Vance jumped up from the couch, and I followed him to the front door. As we stepped outside, we saw someone running from the house. Rocky was hot on their heels, barking furiously.

"Hey!" Vance shouted, trying to get the person to slow down, but they didn't. It was hard to make out any details in the darkness, but as the person disappeared between our house and the neighbor's, they shot a spell over their shoulder. Red sparks erupted, and Rocky yelped in surprise.

"Rocky!" I ran to check on the gargoyle, but Vance held me back.

"Let me go. You watch my back."

I nodded even though there wasn't much I could do. I didn't have my wand on me. My eyes scanned the darkness as Vance rushed over to check on Rocky. "Are you okay, boy?" he asked, examining the gargoyle's wings. Rocky shook his head as if trying to make out what had happened. Good thing gargoyles were tough to curse.

I continued to keep an eye out but didn't see anything other than a broken window on the garage door. Now it matched the other broken window.

I made my way closer to Vance, kicking something in the process. The brown bottle skidded across the driveway. "Is Rocky okay?" I asked as I bent down to look at what I'd kicked.

"Yeah, he's okay. What did you find?"

"I'm not sure. I need a light."

"Are you guys okay?" Jeremy Vanhaven walked over from next door. Our neighbor looked wide awake. He was dressed in black jeans and a dark-colored shirt. I had to admit I was surprised to see him after our last visit. I wouldn't think he'd care, seeing he'd kicked us off his property, but I didn't say anything. Vance went ahead and filled him in on what had happened.

"Did you see anything?" I asked Jeremy.

"No, I just heard you guys. Here." Jeremy pulled out his phone and shined his light on the bottle. It was a bottle of peroxide.

The three of us looked at one another. "I think we need to call the sheriff," I said. Whatever the person was up to, it wasn't good.

As we waited for the sheriff to arrive, Rocky started sniffing around the backyard, hot on the trail of something. It was hard to know what he was after. I wondered if it could be the intruder's scent and if Rocky could track them. But then he climbed the steps to the apartment over the garage and began pawing at the door, clearly wanting to go inside. I exchanged a look with Vance. "Should we let him in?" I'd been inside the apartment before, and nothing had stood out to me, but maybe Rocky knew something we didn't.

"Hang on, I want my wand before we do anything," Vance replied. That was probably a smart idea. "Stay back in case there's someone else in there," Vance said, returning a moment later.

I looked over at Jeremy. I hadn't even thought of that. Now I wished I had my wand too.

"You want backup?" Jeremy asked, following Vance and Rocky up the steps.

"Sure," Vance said over his shoulder.

Rocky stood guard at the door, waiting for Vance to turn the knob.

"On the count of three," Vance whispered. "One, two, three."

Wands at the ready, he turned the doorknob. Rocky barreled inside. I held my breath.

But nothing happened.

"It looks empty," Vance hollered back down to me.

"Okay, that's good." I jogged up the steps to join them. Vance had flipped on the light switch. Two bare bulbs lit up the small room. Rocky zigzagged across the space. His nose was on the ground.

This was the second time I'd been in the one-bedroom apartment. The walls were painted a light pistachio color, and the floor was a beige carpet. There was a small kitchenette in the corner with a sink and a spot for a fridge that was now empty. A single window with tattered curtains would let in a small amount of light when it wasn't boarded up. We were still waiting on Gayle to have it fixed from earlier in the week. The room was mostly empty save for a small sofa against one wall, a coffee table, and a boxy TV from the 1980s. A door off to the side led to a small bathroom. It was a dreary space and looked unremarkable, but Rocky had other ideas. He started digging at the carpet in the corner of the room. At first, he only pawed at it once or twice, but then he started scratching the carpet in earnest.

"What is it, buddy?" Vance asked.

Rocky looked at us over his shoulder. If gargoyles could talk, he'd say, "*Come over here and check this out!*"

The top of the carpet appeared to have a slight stain, or more like the outline of a stain. It was wet. Vance touched the carpet and put his fingers to his nose. "I don't smell anything."

"Is it the peroxide?" I asked. I couldn't remember if peroxide had a smell or not.

"Probably," Vance agreed, pulling back the carpet. When he did, it revealed much more.

Jeremy and I both leaned forward.

"Is that blood?" he asked.

"I think so," Vance remarked. There was a stain on the plywood floor, old and darkened from time. It had seeped into the wood, spreading out like a spider web. It was clear that someone had tried to clean it up, but the stain remained. We stood there momentarily in stunned silence, trying to process what we saw. Rocky continued to sniff around the area. His growls quieted to a low rumble.

Jeremy went home to make sure he shut his back door but said he'd be back to talk to the deputy.

A few minutes later, Sheriff Reynolds and Deputy Amber arrived. Amber looked like she was ready to strangle someone, probably me. "What's so important you dragged us out here in the middle of the night?" she grumbled, rubbing her eyes.

Her father glared at her.

"Sorry, daddy, you know how much I love my sleep."

"And you think someday you want to be sheriff?" The sheriff grunted.

My eyes went wide. Amber as sheriff? That would be a disaster.

The sheriff turned his attention back to us. Together, we gave a rundown of what happened with the intruder and finding the stain. He nodded and then knelt to get a better look. "Looks like blood, all right," he said, his voice grave, "and old. See how it's seeped into the wood here? This didn't happen recently."

"You also found peroxide," Jeremy chimed in, rejoining us.

"Jeremy Vanhaven. What are you doing here?" Sheriff Reynolds eyed our neighbor suspiciously.

"He came outside when Rocky went nuts," I supplied.

"Uh-huh. Pretty convenient, don't you think? What are you doing awake in the middle of the night?"

"I hardly think midnight is the middle of the night," Jeremy replied defensively.

"I suppose we could always ask a judge what he thinks," the sheriff replied.

Jeremy crossed his arms over his chest. "If you're trying to accuse me of something, go on and say it."

The sheriff copied his stance. "No, no accusations. Just trying to figure out how you fit in."

"Not much to figure out. I heard a commotion and came out to see if everything was okay."

"Is that so?" the sheriff asked.

"It is, and if you don't need anything else, I think I'll see myself home." Jeremy shook his head and left without a backward glance.

"There's suspect number one," Amber said with a yawn when Jeremy walked out the door.

I didn't say anything. I wasn't sure how I felt about Jeremy. We hadn't gotten off on the right foot, but then again, we had stopped by his house unannounced and asked about his missing wife. That was probably some sort of social faux pas, but I couldn't deny the facts—his wife was missing, we'd found a woman's skeleton in our backyard, and now, we'd found what looked to be a crime scene in the apartment, perhaps the location that tied it all together. Even I had to admit Jeremy's presence was coincidental, and I generally didn't believe in coincidences. It was all more pieces to the puzzle.

The sheriff turned his attention to me. "I'll have my team come out and process the scene. Keep an eye out on your neighbor and your doors locked."

"Will do," I remarked. Vance nodded the same.

"Did you talk to Sarah's family about the DNA request?"

"No one answered, but I'll call again later today." The sheriff eyed his daughter. Amber was leaning against the wall, looking like she was about to fall asleep standing up. The sheriff shook his head but didn't say another word.

Chapter 15

After the night's excitement, I found myself tossing and turning in bed, unable to settle down. Thankfully, I kept a couple of Connie's calming tonics from the potion shop on hand for the occasion. I slipped out of bed, located one of the tonics in the bathroom cabinet, and quickly downed the contents. The tonic started off cool in my mouth, but it quickly turned warm. Within a few minutes, I felt myself relax, and I drifted off to sleep.

When I woke up the following day, I felt surprisingly refreshed. Vance had already left for work, so I took my time getting ready, thinking about what I wanted to accomplish today. I felt like we were in a holding pattern with Sarah. Until we had a DNA sample, we couldn't match the remains. If they didn't belong to Sarah, I had no idea who they belonged to. If they *did* belong to her, then it would be easy to assume Jeremy had killed her and buried her in the neighbor's backyard, but that didn't explain the blood stain in the garage apartment or why he'd wait until now to destroy the evidence.

I heard a knock on the front door. I wasn't expecting anyone, but I went to answer it anyway. To my surprise, it was Jeremy. It was as if he knew I was thinking about him.

"Can we talk?" he asked.

"Sure. Come on in," I said, opening the door wider.

Rocky was lying on the floor next to me, but as soon as he saw Jeremy, he got up and wagged his long, devil-like tail, bumping his snout into Jeremy's palm to look for pets. Jeremy chuckled, hinting that he liked the gargoyle. I took that as a good sign.

"Sorry to just show up unannounced like this," he said as he followed me into the kitchen. I wordlessly got down two mugs for coffee and held one out.

"No, that's okay. I'm about ready to turn in."

I cocked my head.

"I work nights. Most of my business is out of Shanghai," he explained.

"Oh." That explained why he was up and wide awake last night and why he looked tired when Vance and I had stopped over the one time before. I wasn't sure of the exact time difference, but I was pretty sure it was close to twelve hours.

"I just wanted to come by and…apologize, I guess."

"Apologize?" I repeated, surprised.

"For how I treated you and your husband the other day. I was angry and took it out on you, and that wasn't fair."

I nodded, feeling a little taken aback. "Thank you for saying that. I appreciate it."

Jeremy sat down in one of the chairs at the kitchen table, and Rocky jumped up, putting his oversized paws on Jeremy's lap. Jeremy scratched behind Rocky's ear, and the gargoyle made a happy grunting sound.

"The thing is, everyone's looked at me like I'm guilty since Sarah disappeared, and I honestly have no idea what happened to her. I didn't do anything wrong, but no one believes me. It's made me a bitter person, and I hate it." As Jeremy talked, I could see the pain and desperation in his eyes. I understood that feeling. I knew what it felt like to have people believe the worst about you, to be judged and condemned without evidence, and yet, it didn't seem like Jeremy did much to help his case.

"Why didn't you report her missing?" I asked.

Jeremy shrugged. "She was a writer, and she spent a lot of time on her own. She'd go off for a week or so when she was working. I assumed she just needed space. We'd gotten into a fight a few days before, and she wasn't speaking to me. I wasn't sure if we were headed for divorce, but I loved her. I still do."

"And when she never came back?"

"I didn't know what to think, and then I *couldn't* think about it, not without making myself crazy. Part of me thought maybe she'd moved away and started over somewhere else. I could see her doing that. She hated confrontation. She'd never say what she was thinking. It's one of the things we fought about. I never knew what was going on in her head. I guess I wanted to believe she'd moved away. That's what I've held on to all these years."

I nodded, feeling like Jeremy was deep in denial. I didn't want to point out that her family hadn't heard from her either. She probably would have told them even if she had started over somewhere else.

Then there was the question of magic. Why hadn't Jeremy tried a spell to track her down? "Did you ever perform a tracing spell?" For tracing spells to work, you had to love the person. The stronger your emotions, the stronger the spell. They weren't flawless, and people could cloak their locations, but it was a start.

Jeremy swallowed uncomfortably and shook his head.

"Don't you want to know?" I asked, meaning if Sarah were alive or dead.

Jeremy looked down at Rocky, still wagging his tail, and then back up at me. His eyes locked with mine. Fear stared back at me. "I've been too scared to know the truth."

At that moment, I knew Jeremy hadn't killed his wife. No one could fake that level of raw emotion.

My heart broke for the man, but at the same time, I was frustrated. Frustrated that there were still no answers about Sarah's disappearance after all these years, frustrated Jeremy never even tried to find out what happened to her. I kept those feelings to myself. It wouldn't do me any good to lash out.

My thoughts were interrupted by the base of one of the kitchen pendant lights breaking loose above the center island. The fixture swayed and dropped a few inches. Thankfully, the thick electrical wire kept the fixture from smashing down like the chandelier, but the light now dangled precariously.

"What the—" Jeremy stood abruptly to help.

"Don't worry about it." I waved him away. He looked back at me, seemingly surprised at my blasé attitude. "Don't worry. The house is falling apart. You get used to it."

"Are you sure?" Jeremy continued to stare at the light.

"Positive. I'll take care of it." Vance and I were quickly becoming the hardware store's favorite customers.

I focused back on our conversation. "Listen, I know you're afraid, but I think it's time you faced reality. Something bad happened to Sarah, and you can help us figure out what that was."

"I know. I've been thinking that too." Jeremy looked out into the backyard. "Do you think the body you found is her?"

"I think it's a real possibility. Sheriff Reynolds is contacting her parents to see about a DNA sample."

Jeremy nodded. "If it is her, I don't know what to do. I want justice for her. I want her to rest in peace, but this whole town already thinks I killed her."

"My husband, Vance, is a criminal defense attorney. I promise that if it comes to that, we'll talk with him and work together to uncover the truth."

Jeremy blew out a shaky breath, and I could tell his emotions were about to overcome him.

"We'll be in touch, okay?"

Jeremy nodded. "Thank you. For everything." He left right after that.

Shortly after, I climbed onto the counter to try and secure the light. To my astonishment, the base had never even been screwed in place. There weren't any holes in the drywall. I wasn't sure who'd overseen the home improvements here, but they were awful.

After screwing the fixture properly in place, I decided to search the house to see if Harriet kept old records of who rented the apartment. Perhaps the bloodstain wasn't related to the body in the backyard, and a former tenant might know what it was about. I wanted to explore all the options in case we hit another dead end.

I started searching through the remaining boxes in the garage, but unfortunately, I didn't find any formal leases or rental agreements. Next, I searched the main house, up high in the closets and the kitchen cupboards. I came across an old wedding album and family pictures as I searched. I knew Harriet's sister, Gayle, would return to town in a few days, and I wanted to give her these sentimental items. I set them aside.

"What's this?" While searching in the cupboard above the refrigerator, I stumbled upon an old dusty book. It was behind a bottle of expired cooking sherry. I had to stand on my tiptoes to reach it. I brought it down and blew on the cover, revealing the title, *101 Spells to Fix Up Your House*. "You've got to be kidding me." I leafed through the pages. The book contained a variety of spells for different house repairs: everything from fixing leaky pipes to restoring creaky floorboards and installing lighting. The book claimed no skills were required, and the spells promised lasting results. I eyed the house suspiciously. Were these spells the reason the place seemed to be falling apart? It was an intriguing thought; I'd bring it up with Vance.

Unfortunately, my morning sleuthing session had to end there. I needed to meet Diane at the bakery to discuss birthday cake. I hadn't forgotten about Aunt Thelma's upcoming birthday, but I hadn't done anything to prepare for it either. I still hadn't located a calligrapher, and I'd have to get on it soon if we would get the invitations out on time. Thank goodness it was still a month away.

Chapter 16

I sat at a small table in the bakery, sampling different cake flavors with Diane. The bakery was quiet mid-morning, with only a few customers coming in for coffee and pastries. As we sipped on coffee and tried out different samples, I mentioned the magical house-fixing book I had found earlier. Diane listened as I explained my suspicions that the spells in the book were responsible for the odd occurrences in the house.

She nodded in agreement. "I think you're right. The charms Harriet put on the house probably quit working after she passed away, and the effects are slowly wearing off."

As I took a bite of lemon cake, I noticed Connie walking in. The potion shop owner smiled and waved before ordering a coffee at the counter. After getting her drink, she joined us.

"Hey, Connie, how are you?" I asked.

"Good, good. Just needed a little caffeine boost this morning," Connie replied, sipping her coffee. "I heard about the bones in your backyard. Any luck solving the case?"

"Yes, and no. Every time I think we're on the right track, it ends up being a dead end." I filled Connie in on solving Luella's missing person case, the possible new lead with Sarah's family's DNA, and the fact that someone broke into the garage apartment last night.

"Whoever the killer is, they're still in town," Diane surmised.

"You might want to stop by and get a protection potion again," Connie offered. Connie's potion had saved me before. It only protected you from magical attacks, but anything was better than nothing.

"That's a good idea. I'll stop by after we're done here if that works for you?"

"Absolutely." Connie thought for a moment. "You know, come to think of it, I dated a guy that rented that garage apartment."

"You did? When was that?" I asked.

"Oh, years ago; fifteen, at least. We were young, or make that, I was. Young and dumb. I thought I knew it all when I was in my twenties. The guy was a total jerk. I only went out with him one time. Let me think. What was his name?" Connie tapped her chin. "Gavin… something. He lost his temper at dinner, and I never talked to him again. I found out later he had a record for assault."

My mind was racing with the possibilities. Could Gavin be responsible for the blood stain in the apartment? Was it possible that he still lived in the area?

"Gavin Brown, that's it! It's all coming back to me. A few months after our date, he got into a fight with Gerald, and he kicked him out. Last I heard, he lived out in The Crossroads, but that was years ago."

We all made a face at that. The Crossroads, a unique magical community, wasn't your typical tourist destination. They didn't care for Silverlake's cheerful atmosphere but instead preferred to embrace their reputation as a group of outcasts and misfits. Most of its members were shapeshifters who'd been cast out of their packs with rogue witches thrown in for fun. I once visited The Cross-roads in high school for a bonfire. I quickly realized I wasn't as cool as I thought. The place had given me the creeps, and I was sure I'd been watched the entire time by invisible eyes. I wasn't excited to interview Gavin Brown at The Crossroads, but a witch did what she had to do.

"You better not head out there alone." Diane gave me a leveled stare.

"Don't worry. I won't." This wasn't going to be a suicide mission.

AFTER STOPPING by Connie's shop for the protection potion, I wasn't sure who to call to head out with me to interview Gavin. I didn't want to pull Vance away from work, Aunt Thelma would try and talk me out of it, and Clemmie would probably cause trouble. That left Misty. I crossed my fingers she was free.

But before I called her, I needed to do some research. Luckily, I knew one decent person with ties to The Crossroads, and hopefully, he could help. Mr. Skylar was the high school history teacher in Silverlake. He grew up in The Crossroads and still tutored out there, trying to make a difference.

I called the high school and waited while the secretary put me through to Mr. Skylar's classroom.

"Mr. Skylar," the history teacher said above the din of the classroom.

"Hey, Mr. Skylar, what about number twenty-one?" A student asked before I could even say hello.

"Hang on, Mason," Mr. Skylar replied.

I felt guilty for interrupting but I needed to ask him a quick question. "Hey, it's Angelica Blackwell. Sorry for interrupting, but I'm working on a case and have a quick question. Do you know Gavin Brown from The Crossroads?"

There was a brief pause before he responded, "I know *of* him. He's a mechanic and keeps to himself."

"Do you know which house is his?"

"I do, but not sure he'd appreciate you stopping by."

"That's a given," I laughed. No one at The Crossroads like outsiders stopping by.

"I forgot you know how it is out there. Alright then, his house is at the end of the main road. It dead-ends at it. Bunch of broken-down cars in the front yard. You can't miss it."

"Okay, thanks." At least now, I had a starting point for my interview.

"If he asks, you didn't get directions from me."

"Got it. My lips are sealed."

"Mr. Skylar! Mr. Skylar!" Another student called out, or maybe it was the same student. It was hard to tell.

I wrapped up the call. "Thanks for your help. I'll talk to you later."

Next, I connected with Misty.

"Just give me twenty minutes," she said after I explained the situation. Misty was always more adventurous than me. In fact, it was because of her that I had been at the infamous bonfire party years ago.

"Okay, I'll swing by and pick you up."

"It's a date!"

As I hung up the phone, I smiled. I was thankful to have a friend like Misty. She was always willing to dive headfirst into a mystery. Sometimes, quicker than me.

AS SOON AS we crossed the last four-way stop that marked the beginning of The Crossroads, the air crackled with magic. I felt a familiar hum in my veins as my power responded to the shift in the atmosphere. We turned onto a narrow, unpaved road, where the grass and dirt kicked up behind us. There were no official markers welcoming us into the neighborhood. It was as if the outcasts had formed an outpost, and a makeshift neighborhood sprung up around it. The houses were a motley collection, ranging from small family homes and doublewides with detached garages to sheds with tarps for roofs and corrugated metal sides.

Gavin's house was at the end of a long, winding dirt road. The front yard was littered with rusted car parts and broken-down vehicles. Dead grass poked through the dirt, giving the impression that it hadn't seen water in quite some time. The porch was cluttered with stacks of newspapers and old tools. The windows were dirty and looked like they hadn't been cleaned in years.

"Connie dated this guy?" Misty asked, looking at the house.

"Once. Did I mention he was previously charged with assault?"

"Don't worry. I'll have my wand at the ready."

"Okay, let's go then."

As usual, I could feel people watching me even though I didn't see anyone as we approached the house. It was eerily silent, as if even nature had avoided the place. Misty and I walked up to the porch, keeping alert to our surroundings. Misty rang the doorbell, but it didn't even make a sound. I knocked on the door instead.

The silence stretched on. Not even a dog barked.

The air felt heavy as we stood there on the doorstep. I eyed Misty, wondering if she could feel it too. Some people put wards on their homes to make people stay away. At that moment, I would've sworn Gavin had done the same.

"Can I help you?" The man's voice came from behind us.

"AH!" I jumped.

Misty and I whipped around, wands raised.

The man chuckled. "You can take your best shot. Doubt it will do much." He was a big man with a gruff appearance that made him look like some type of shifter, probably a grizzly bear.

"Sorry, you startled us. We're looking for Gavin Brown. Is that you?" I asked.

"It sure is, ma'am. What can I do for you?" Gavin asked, his voice deep but gentle.

His manners took me by surprise.

I took a second to compose my thoughts, apologizing yet again.

"What's this about now? Are you all right?" Gavin seemed genuinely concerned for Misty and me.

I took a deep breath, trying to hide my nervousness. "We're investigating an old case, and we were wondering if you remember renting a garage apartment from the Moonstones about fifteen years ago?"

Gavin scratched his chin, deep in thought. "Yeah, I remember the Moonstones. Harriet was a nice lady. How she doing?"

"Unfortunately, she passed away a few months back," I explained.

"Sorry to hear that. Harriet took me in when no one else would give me a chance. She saw the good in me. I was different back then," Gavin went on to explain. "Always angry and quick to fight."

Gavin's comment about fighting was a natural segue. "Did you ever get into a fight in the apartment?" I asked.

"Like a fistfight?" Gavin asked.

"Mm-hm. We found an old bloodstain in the apartment. Trying to figure out where it came from."

"And a skeleton in the backyard," Misty added.

I eyed my best friend. I wasn't going to tell him that unless I had to.

"You're wondering if I had anything to do with it seeing as I used to rough people up a bit?" Gavin asked, trying to piece it all together.

"No," I said while Misty replied, "yes."

I spoke over my friend. "I was wondering if you knew anything about it. The two might not be related. The bloodstain is old, and who knows how long the bones have been there, but you're the only person I know who's rented the apartment, so I thought it was worth a shot." I was babbling, I knew that, and yet I couldn't stop.

"Ah, well, to answer your question, yes, I know about the bloodstain."

"You do?" I wasn't expecting that.

"I'm the one who replaced the carpet. Mrs. Moonstone let me stay at the apartment for free in exchange for me fixing the place up. It was a great deal."

"There was a big blood stain on the floor, and she never said anything?" Misty asked.

"No, there was a big bleached-out mark on the carpeting, but when I ripped it up, you could see the blood stain in the padding and subfloor. Mrs. Moonstone had no idea what it was about, so we just put the new carpet on top."

I was trying to piece everything together. If the bloodstain had been there fifteen years ago, it wasn't connected to Sarah's disappearance. She'd only been missing for five years. The stain could be a random accident, after all.

"Hmmm, okay, well, that's helpful. Thank you so much."

"That's what I like to hear," Gavin replied.

We turned to leave, but then I stopped. "One more question. Why did you move out if it was such a great deal?"

"That's easy. Gerald didn't like having another man on his property. I managed to fix up the bathroom and put down the carpet before he kicked me out."

Misty and I exchanged a look. It seemed like everyone had a history with Gerald. We needed to pivot our investigation to him. Only I didn't know where to start.

———————————————

Chapter 17

———————————————

That night, Percy agreed to go ghost hunting with me. I didn't have anything else to do. Vance was busy pulling background information on Gerald, and the sheriff was working overtime on Sarah's DNA test. He spoke with Sarah's family that afternoon and obtained a DNA sample from her parents. I figured it couldn't hurt to try and help the ghost at Craddock House in the meantime.

According to Gabby, the woman was usually found near the apple orchard or the backyard's hedge maze.

"Here, take the ranger," Gabby said, tossing me a set of keys. "It'll make it easier to get around the property."

I readily took her up on the offer. "Thanks." Tonight was the perfect ghost-hunting weather. The fog rolled in across the lake and hills. Clouds blotted out the moon. The air was thick with moisture and felt like it might rain any minute.

Ghosts didn't bother me. Heck, one was even coming with me to talk to the mysterious woman, but still, I was nervous. Why? Because ghosts were unpredictable. You never knew if they would jump out at you, throw something at your head, or lead you into a trap.

I thought we should start furthest away from the house before it started raining. As we drove out to the orchard, I eyed the various structures around the property. We came across the old barn, which used to house livestock, and the carriage house, which had been converted into a guesthouse. There was also a pump house and a few smaller sheds. I'd explore those in the daylight.

Percy and I kept our eyes peeled as we approached the apple orchard for any sign of the ghost.

"Here, ghostie, ghostie! Here, ghostie, ghostie!" Percy whistled.

I eased off the gas and turned to my companion. "Are you kidding me?"

"What? I don't know her name, do you?"

"No," I prolonged the word, "but do you think she will reply to that call?"

Percy snickered. "Why, yes. Yes, I do."

Suddenly, I saw a faint glow in the distance. Unless Craddock House had another ghost on the property, it was her. The woman's features and clothes were unclear, but her glowing partial form was unmistakable.

I got out of the ranger and started walking on foot. "Hello?" I called out to the woman. I knew she heard me because she looked in my direction. "We're not here to hurt you. We just want to talk."

The woman's glow flickered, and she seemed to waver in the air, but in the next instant, she disappeared.

"Where'd she go?" I looked around the orchard, but it was hard to see much in front of me.

"Hang on. I'll get her!"

"Wait!"

But Percy had already disappeared.

The next minute was chaotic, with the woman popping up over by this tree and that tree with Percy right on her proverbial heels. Maybe bringing the poltergeist wasn't a good idea. I thought having another ghost with me would give me street credit, but it looked like I'd been wrong.

"Get back here, ghostie. We have some questions for you!" Percy demanded.

"Percy, stop!" I shouted. "She won't talk to us if you keep chasing her!"

Percy didn't listen to me. He was relentless in trying to catch the woman.

"Stop disappearing!" Percy shouted in frustration.

I quickly realized tonight was a bust. The ghost did not like Percy (not that I could blame her), and she wasn't about to stop and chat with us. The next time I came out, it was going to be alone.

"Come on, Percy. Let's go." I walked back to the UTV.

"What? We just got here. She's gonna get tired sooner or later."

"But I want her to like us."

"Like us? Why? I thought you wanted answers?" Percy looked genuinely confused.

"We've got time. Don't worry about it."

Percy sighed. "You never let me have any fun."

"Oh, come now. How about I give you back your whoopee cushion? Does that sound like fun?"

"And my fake snake?"

"Don't push it."

I WOKE WITH A START. I immediately felt like someone was watching me. My heart rate began to pick up, and my mind raced with the possibilities. Did someone break in? I was frozen in bed, listening carefully. The house was dead silent. I didn't hear any footsteps or creaking floorboards.

I glanced over at Vance, sleeping soundly next to me. His even breathing reassured me that I was probably just paranoid, but I still couldn't shake the feeling that someone or something was watching me.

I took a deep breath and tried to calm down, but the feeling of being watched didn't go away. It lingered like a heavy weight on my chest, and I couldn't shake it off.

I slowly sat up in bed, listening to the sounds of the night. The wind outside was picking up, making the tree branches scrape against the windows. Outside, an owl hooted in the distance. But there was something else—unease slowly crept up on me.

Getting out of bed, I tiptoed to the window and peered out into the darkness. The moon was hidden behind the clouds, casting an eerie glow over the yard. Everything was quiet. Too quiet.

Suddenly, movement caught my eye. There, in the shadows of the trees, was a figure. I strained my eyes, trying to determine who or what it was. Then as if sensing my gaze, the figure turned and looked up at me. It was the ghost from Craddock House.

I stood in place, watching her. She didn't move or speak. She just looked up at me with sad, pleading eyes. Then, in the blink of an eye, she was gone.

I stood there momentarily, trying to process what had just happened. Was the Craddock House ghost tied to the case I was working on? Could the spirit be Sarah Vanhaven's, or was she someone else? Someone unrelated who also needed my help?

I made a mental note to research the history of Craddock House and its former residents in the morning. Until then, I needed to take a deep breath and calm my nerves. I wouldn't find the answers tonight.

Chapter 18

The following day, my phone rang as I poured my first cup of coffee. It was Sheriff Reynolds.

"Good morning," I said when answering.

"Maybe for you, but it's not here."

"Don't say that. What now?" I sat down at the kitchen table with my cup of coffee.

"The DNA from Sarah's parents isn't a match."

"What? I was hoping we'd finally get an ID."

"I know. Me too. But she's not our victim. There's zero probability."

I let out a sigh of disappointment.

"But here's the thing, you're right; someone doesn't want this case solved."

"How so?"

"There was a break-in at the department last night. Luckily, Dr. Fitz was working late and scared them off."

"Did you get them on camera?"

The sheriff was quiet. I wasn't sure if we would ever answer me. Finally, he said, "No. They haven't been working lately."

"I see." I remembered Dottie mentioning something to Vance about that earlier in the week.

"Don't worry. I'm fixing it now. In the meantime, keep an eye out. Jane Doe's killer is definitely someone still here in Silverlake."

I reassured the sheriff we were being safe. The sheriff's caution also reminded me to swallow a mouthful of Connie's protection potion. I should've had Vance do the same before he left this morning, but I'd been too busy telling him about last night's paranormal visit and how I thought the ghost might belong to Sarah Vanhaven. It looked like that theory was worthless now.

I thanked the sheriff for the update and hung up, feeling conflicted. It's not that I wanted the remains to belong to Sarah, but I wanted answers.

I also needed to update Jeremy on the latest development with the case. Even though he slept days, I figured he'd want to hear the news immediately. I headed next door and knocked on his door. After a few moments, he answered, looking groggy and disheveled.

"What's wrong?" he asked.

"Sorry to wake you, but there's been news."

Jeremy braced himself on the doorframe, his knuckles turning white as he gripped it for support.

I didn't waste any time relaying the message. "The remains aren't Sarah's."

Jeremy deflated like a balloon pricked with a pin. "Thank you," he said to the sky.

I replied with a soft, empathetic smile.

"Do you they know *who* they belong to?" Jeremy asked after a moment.

"No, and we obviously still don't know what happened to Sarah."

"I'm not sure I can live like this anymore, that I want to live like this anymore." Jeremy's words were heavy with sorrow, each syllable a testament to his ongoing pain.

"I can understand that." I thought about what I'd do if Vance was missing. I knew the answer. I would scour the earth until I found him, my determination fueled by a love that knew no bounds.

Jeremy's case was different. They were estranged when Sarah went missing. He thought she left on her own accord. Now, so much time has passed, and the leads have gone cold. It would take a miracle or a hefty dose of magic to uncover the truth.

"I'm ready to try the tracing spell," Jeremy said with determination before I could even suggest it. "If it can help us discover what happened to Sarah, then it's worth a shot."

"That was my next idea." I didn't know the

perimeters of a tracing spell. Would it work if Sarah were deceased? What about if she were on the other side of the world?

While Jeremy got cleaned up for the day, I called my aunt to get her opinion, relaying my concerns.

"You're right; it might not work," she said flatly.

"Aunt Thelma! That's not what I want to hear."

"Okay, alright, let me think on this."

I waited impatiently on the other end of the line as she mulled over the situation.

"Ah, I have an idea. Does Jeremy still have any of Sarah's personal belongings? Something important to her, maybe?"

"I'm not sure, but I can ask him."

"Do that. It'll help strengthen the spell."

"Got it. What else?"

"Now, how much magic is Jeremy packing?"

"Huh?"

"How powerful is he?"

"Oh, I have no idea." He could be a shifter for all I knew. Of course, the spell wouldn't work if he was.

"In that case, I suggest we all get together to work the spell. Want me to make some calls?"

"Sure, yeah, that would be great." Hopefully, Jeremy would be okay with that.

"Okay, then, let me see what I can do. I'll call you back."

"Thank you. Talk soon." I called Vance next.

He said he'd be free to come home and help in an hour. After that, I found myself pacing the floor, unsure of what else to do.

Jeremy arrived first, and I explained the situation. "My aunt thinks it would be best if we all worked together on this tracing spell. She's going to make some calls to see if anyone else can join us."

"Okay," Jeremy said, seeming as nervous as I felt. "What do I need to do?"

"My aunt suggested we use something of Sarah's to add power to the spell, something important to her. Do you have anything like that?"

Jeremy looked thoughtful for a moment. "I have her wedding ring. She left it on the dresser the morning she disappeared. It's another reason why I thought she left on purpose. Would that work?"

"I think so."

"Okay, I'll go get it."

IT TURNED out we couldn't all get together until that evening. Jeremy was okay with that. Seeing as he waited five years to perform the spell, what was another couple of hours?

One by one, my friends and family arrived until there were seven of us: Jeremy, Vance, Aunt Thelma, Clemmie, Misty, Daniel, and me. I considered that a good sign. Seven was, after all, a magical number.

We gathered in the backyard under the full moon. Jeremy held Sarah's wedding ring tightly while I led the group in casting the circle. Aunt Thelma sprinkled herbs around the edge, creating a protective barrier. Vance and Daniel set up candles around the circle's perimeter, adding their energy to the mix. Clemmie and Misty held hands and closed their eyes, focusing their minds on the task at hand.

"Okay, everyone, let's begin," Aunt Thelma said, taking a deep breath. "We're going to try and trace Sarah's energy using her wedding ring. Jeremy, can you hold the ring in front of you, please?"

He nodded and extended his arm, holding the ring toward the circle's center. I could feel the energy in the air, the power of the moon, and the collective magic of our group. I closed my eyes and focused, reaching out with my magic to connect with the group. Aunt Thelma held out her wand and whispered an incantation. I felt the magic within our circle intensify.

"Visualize Sarah's energy flowing from the ring," Aunt Thelma said, her voice low and calm. "Picture it like a thread leading us to her."

The air around us seemed to shimmer and shift as if the very fabric of reality was bending to our will. I could sense the energy flowing from the ring, a faint shimmering aura extending into the night.

"Follow the thread," she said with her voice barely above a whisper. "Let it guide us to her."

In my mind, I lifted off the ground and started flying. The earth blurred below me, and the air whipped my hair back. Suddenly, I was transported back inside Craddock House. I have no idea if everyone else saw what I saw, and I don't dare to stop and ask.

Images flickered before me, and I felt like I was seeing things from Sarah's perspective. She was looking for something inside the house, shining her flashlight around the formal living room in the darkness of night. She moved slowly, cautiously, sneaking around the room, picking up a vase, and inspecting it before turning her attention to a large painting above the mantel.

As Sarah inspected each item, her heart beat faster with anticipation. She was looking for something specific, but I didn't know what. Sarah picked up a few more pieces, a bronze horse not more than a foot tall from the side table, followed by a porcelain vase on the mantel. Each time she turned the piece over and examined the bottoms of them. Sarah moved from the living room to the library, still searching, her eyes darting around the room. She walked toward a painting. It was an impressionist piece with swirling brushstrokes that captured the essence of the French countryside. It depicted a field of poppies, their bright red petals contrasting against the lush green of the grass. In the distance, a small cottage could be seen, nestled among the trees. The sky was a riot of blues and purples, with fluffy white clouds floating lazily by. Sarah's flashlight focused on the signature at the bottom.

Suddenly, a spell hit her from behind. She was blindsided. *I* was blindsided. It was as if I were experiencing the effects myself. I sensed the weight of my own body as I became heavier and heavier, as if I were being pulled down into the ground. My thoughts became sluggish and distorted. I tried to scream, but my voice was trapped inside me. I could feel my insides hardening and my skin turning into concrete. I couldn't move. Like a victim of Medusa, I'd been turned into stone.

The next thing I knew, I was back with the group, gasping for air.

My heart was pounding, and my hands were shaking. I took a moment to catch my breath and steady myself. "I think I know where she is or where she was," I said, facing the others. "Sarah, I mean. She was attacked inside Craddock House, and she might still be alive."

Chapter 19

I filled the team in on what I had experienced. They listened intently as I recounted what I had seen and felt.

"It was like I was Sarah, searching for something in the darkness, and then someone snuck up on me, and it was lights out," I said, shuddering at the memory.

Vance put a hand on my shoulder, his expression one of concern. "Are you sure you're okay?"

"Yeah, I think so." I took a deep breath. "But I think we need to go to Craddock House." I had no idea why she'd been turned into a statue or who had done it, but I felt confident that's what happened to her. Thankfully, stone spells could usually be reversed. I just hoped that was the case for Sarah.

We walked up to the front door, and Gabby was

there to greet us. She looked surprised to see us but welcomed us into the house.

"You think someone was attacked here?" she asked as I recounted the story.

"Yes, but it was before your time here, about five years ago."

"You don't think my grandfather...." Gabby let her voice trail off.

"No, I don't think he was involved. I can't imagine how." Gabby's grandfather had been a kind man. I couldn't see him turning Sarah into a statue.

"Your family's art collection is still scattered throughout the house, right?" I asked Gabby.

"Yes, but there's no life-sized statues," Gabby said.

"She could've been shrunk," Clemmie offered up.

I grimaced. Jeremy's face looked ashen. I had thought the same thing as Clemmie but hadn't wanted to say it. Almost every witch had a minimizing charm in their arsenal.

"How about we split up? It might be easier to search that way," Vance offered.

"I'll check my bedroom just to be sure there isn't something I've overlooked," Gabby replied.

The rest of us divided the house up, but with over six thousand square feet, including an attic and a basement, this would take a while. I debated trying a summoning charm, but it wouldn't work without knowing exactly what the statue looked like.

We started searching the house from top to bottom. We looked in every room, nook, and cranny, but we couldn't find anything resembling a statue. It was like trying to find a needle in a haystack.

As we searched, I became less optimistic.

"Just because she was attacked here doesn't mean she's still here," Vance said as we combed the attic.

"I know. It was a long shot." If the attacker minimized the statue, she could be anywhere, maybe even in a museum. I shuddered at the thought, but then I thought of something. "Hang on, where's Jeremy?"

"I think in the basement with Gabby."

"Let's go find him. I have an idea. Do you remember the ghost I told you about?" Vance nodded. "Gabby said it seemed like she wanted someone to follow her. Maybe she knows where Sarah is." The possibility, however slim, was worth exploring.

"Okay, I say it's worth a shot."

"But I think only Jeremy and I should go. She seems shy. Not sure she'll reveal herself if everyone's outside." The thought of potentially scaring off our only lead was too great a risk to take.

Vance agreed, and we rounded up the group to

explain the plan. They seemed skeptical but ultimately supportive, knowing that we didn't have many other options.

Ten minutes later, Jeremy and I stepped outside, trying to connect with the ghost of Craddock House. I didn't think she was Sarah's ghost, but I still hoped she could help us. We started walking toward the apple orchard. The wind picked up, causing the leaves to rustle and the branches to sway, but something else was in the air, a sense of presence that was hard to describe.

"Can you hear me?" I spoke softly into the wind, my breath visible in unnaturally cold air.

"Can you help us?" Jeremy spoke up, his voice low and soothing. "We're looking for my wife." His desperation was palpable.

Suddenly, a gust of wind whipped around us, causing our hair to whip around our faces. I felt a chill run down my spine but stood my ground. I was determined to discover the truth no matter what.

"We won't hurt you," I promised, trying to convey sincerity and warmth in my tone.

There was a moment of silence, and then, we heard a faint whisper in the wind. It was hard to make out at first, but as we listened carefully, the voice became clearer. "Peace," the ghost whispered. "Give me peace." Her plea was haunting.

Suddenly, a purple floating orb materialized before us. It hovered around us briefly before moving slowly back toward the house. I wasn't sure what was happening, but I felt like we needed to follow it.

"Come on, let's see where she goes," I told Jeremy.

The orb led us to the hedge maze, disappearing inside the labyrinth of green. We followed it, my heart pounding with anticipation.

The maze was an intricate network of pathways and walls made entirely from carefully trimmed bushes and hedges. It was tall enough to block the view of the outside world, making it feel like a separate world within the boundaries of the Craddock estate. The bushes were neatly trimmed, and the path was narrow, forcing those who entered to take slow, deliberate steps. The air was thick with the scent of freshly cut hedges, and every twist and turn revealed a sight to behold, like a beautiful rose bush or a peaceful sitting area.

As we neared the maze's center, we spotted a gazebo, and behind that stood a statue in the corner. A sense of recognition washed over me. It was Sarah, her face frozen in a serene expression, her body preserved in stone.

I KNEW we needed to help Sarah and transform her back, but it wouldn't be me. I didn't want to take any chances and leave her permanently stuck. Five years was plenty long enough. I called Sheriff Reynolds and filled him in on the situation, explaining how we'd found her. The sheriff agreed it was best to leave Sarah's condition to the professionals and said he'd call Cassidy, one of the town's healers, and Dr. Fitz to help with her medical care. I felt relieved knowing we had a plan to help Sarah and that we wouldn't attempt to reverse the spell ourselves.

When the paramedics arrived, Jeremy stayed by his wife's side and went with her to the hospital. He promised to call us when she was transformed back and awake. I really wanted to interview her and find out how much she remembered. Why was she sneaking around Craddock House? What was she looking for? There was still so much I didn't know, but I wouldn't rush her. She's been through an Ordeal with a capital O.

"That's two cases you've solved this week," Aunt Thelma said, raising her glass to me. We had regrouped down at the tavern.

"But not the original one I'd set out to," I countered, clinking my glass to hers anyway.

"Who do you think the remains belong to?" Misty asked, taking a swig of her beer.

"My money was on Sarah. I still can't believe she was a statue this whole time," Clemmie interrupted.

"I know, and you thought Jeremy had killed her," Aunt Thelma remarked.

"Oh, like you didn't!" Clemmie countered.

"Who's this Craddock House ghost Misty was telling me about?" Daniel asked, interrupting my aunt and Clemmie's squabble.

"Good question. A couple of ghost hunters are staying at the inn—" I started to say.

"You mean they *were* staying at the inn," Aunt Thelma commented.

"What happened?" I asked. "Last I heard, they weren't going anywhere."

"We told Percy to leave them alone. I mean, we all did remember? Did he listen? No. He made their entire bed levitate, tossed their suitcases around the room, and told them to get out."

"He did not!" Misty said before I could.

"You don't have to worry about them returning," Clemmie quipped.

"Would you if you were a mortal?" Aunt Thelma replied.

"Nope, no, ma'am," Clemmie replied.

"It's their fault. They started talking in the lobby about offering ghost tours to mortals, setting up shop right here in Silverlake, and bringing mortals in by the busloads." My aunt shook her head.

I guess that was one way to get rid of our potential ghost-hunter problem, although it would've been nicer to erase their memories. "Anyway, the ghost hunters were the ones who told me about her. She's another case we need to solve, I think."

"What do you mean 'you think'?" Misty asked.

"Well, when she helped Jeremy and me tonight, she said, *'give me peace.'*"

"Like she wants you to leave her alone, or she's not at peace?" Vance asked.

"I'm not sure," I confessed.

"What made you think to ask her in the first place?" Daniel asked.

"It was a hunch. Gabby said the ghost would try and get her to follow her, but she never did. I thought maybe she knew a secret she wanted to share."

"Maybe finding Sarah brought her peace?" Misty suggested.

I shrugged. I had no idea.

Chapter 20

I couldn't believe it had been over a week since Rocky discovered the remains in our backyard. I could usually solve cases in a handful of days. I didn't like that this one was taking me so long.

That afternoon, Sheriff Reynolds called while I was working the front desk at the inn.

"Good news," he said when I answered. "Sarah's awake."

"She is? That's great. How is she?"

"Stable, but she doesn't remember much," he replied.

"Does she know why she was at Craddock House?"

"No, and she doesn't know who attacked her either."

"Well, at the least she's okay."

"It's a start. Dr. Fitz thinks her memory will come back to her in time."

"I hope he's right."

"You and me both. Listen, there's something else I want to talk to you about. Those remains in your backyard? I got the lab analysis back. They've been buried for a couple of decades at least."

"That long ago?"

"Uh-huh."

I twisted my lips while I thought. "Do you know of any other missing person cases from that time?"

"I sure don't. I have Amber back downstairs looking, but so far, she hasn't come up with anything." I bet Amber loved that.

"Okay, well, I'll let you know if we have any other leads." Vance had dug up plenty of complaints against Gerald. The only problem was most of those people had since passed away. I'd say we were flat out of leads.

I hung up with the sheriff and got back to work.

I looked up an hour later and smiled as Harriet's sister, Gayle, walked in the door.

"Thought you might be here. I stopped by the house, but no one was home."

"You're right. If I'm not there, I'm usually here. How are you?"

"Good. I wanted to get back and check on the house. I felt bad taking off on a case like that."

"No need to apologize. I know how that goes. But I'm glad you're here. I need to talk with you."

"What's wrong?" Gayle must've known it wasn't good by the tone of my voice.

"First, before I forget, I found a wedding album and some family photos at the house. I wanted to return them to you."

"Oh, sorry about that."

"That's okay." I looked over at the clock. "Vance will be home in an hour if you want to swing by and pick them up."

"I'll go ahead and do that."

"Next, do you know if your sister used a spell book to fix up the house?"

Gayle's face fell. "Oh, no. Tell me she didn't."

"I think she did because the house seems to be falling apart."

Gayle sighed. "That doesn't surprise me at all. I told her not to do it. You can't cut corners when it comes to home repairs. How bad is it?"

I ran through the list of things that had gone wrong in the past week. Unfortunately, we had no idea what other charms might soon wear off.

"Rest assured, I'll send a contractor over and make sure everything's put to rights, even if it costs me a fortune. Don't worry. The estate can afford it."

"Really?" Harriet and Gerald didn't strike me as the wealthy type.

"Gerald must have been the cheapest man alive.

Heaven knows he was the grumpiest." Gayle scowled.

"That's something else I wanted to talk to you about." I waited for a young family to make their way to the elevators before continuing. "We found a skeleton buried in the backyard."

Gayle's expression changed from shock to disbelief. "What now? Are you joking?"

"I wish I was. We've been tracking down leads, but so far, they haven't led us anywhere."

"You don't know who it is?"

"No, ma'am. We know it's a woman, and since her discovery, I've solved two cold cases."

"Well, that's something. You ever think about a career in law enforcement? The Agency could use a clever witch like you."

I smiled. "I'm flattered, really, but I'm happy solving crimes in my little corner of the world here."

"Suit yourself. Regardless, I'll call my boss and see if he can spare me a few days so I can help you out with this. That okay with you?"

"Yeah. We can use all the help we can get." Especially from an experienced agent like Gayle.

Gayle nodded. "Guess I need a room then."

"Okay, let's get you checked in then."

LATER THAT AFTERNOON, the team met up at Clemmie's tea shop to discuss the latest developments in the case. Clemmie had closed the shop early so we could have the place to ourselves. Aunt Thelma, Misty, Vance, and Gayle were all there, ready to dive into the discussion.

We sat at a round table, sipping on Clemmie's latest blend of tea, a combination of chamomile and lavender that was supposed to help with relaxation, but I could tell by the tension in the air that we were all far from relaxed.

"So, what's the latest?" Clemmie asked, leaning forward in her chair.

I filled everyone in on what the sheriff had told me earlier in the day about Sarah being transformed back into human form but not remembering much about her time as a statue. We also knew the remains had been buried in the ground for at least twenty years.

Gayle shook her head. "I just can't believe my sister was involved in something like this, but Gerald on the other hand..."

"That's what everyone says," I agreed.

"Could he have had an affair?" Misty asked.

"And then killed her when things went south?" Vance added

Gayle made a face. "I can't see anyone wanting to have an affair with Gerald. Half the time, I thought he bewitched my sister into staying married to him. Heaven knows what she saw in him."

"Your sister ever mention any side hanky panky?" Aunt Thelma asked.

"No, definitely not. Neither one of them," Gayle confirmed.

"Cross torrid affair off the list." Clemmie slashed " X " with her finger in the air.

"Earlier, I'd tried to find records of past renters, thinking one might be the victim or the killer, but I couldn't find any. Do you know if your sister kept contracts or payment records?"

"Harriet keep records? Unlikely. She was more about helping people get back on their feet. I'm sure half the people stayed there for free. Sorry, I know that's not much help."

"What about Craddock House? Sarah was attacked there five years ago. Why?" Misty asked.

"And is it connected to the remains?" Aunt Thelma asked.

"Now, you're talking," Clemmie agreed. "We need to explore that angle."

"It would help if Sarah remembered something," I remarked. The images from last night, when I'd experienced Sarah's attack, replayed through my mind. "She was searching for something like maybe an antique or a painting. I don't think even she knew."

"What makes you say that?" Gayle asked.

I scrunched my brow in thought. "She picked up items and looked at the bottom of them. With the paintings, her light focused on the signature."

"Maybe we should head back to Craddock House and catalog the artwork?" Vance suggested.

"Not a bad idea. I'd also look at the household staff," Gayle suggested.

I looked over at my aunt and Clemmie. "Does Gabby employ anyone?"

"I assume she doesn't maintain that property all by herself, but I don't know who's running things these days," Aunt Thelma replied.

Clemmie snapped her fingers. "What about Caroline? She used to be the housekeeper."

"I don't think she's doing too well. I saw her at Silver Wand when I was playing bridge with Boyd. She couldn't follow suit no matter how many times we reminded her. Doubt she'll remember much from five years ago," Aunt Thelma replied.

Aunt Thelma's remarks about Caroline's memory reminded me to check in with Mrs. Potts and track down her family. I still needed to do that. "I'll pop in and talk with Caroline. I'd like to tell Boyd we solved Luella's case anyway."

"While you do that, I'll go around Gerald's old haunts and see what I can drum up. An old buddy or two might have some dirt to spill," Gayle offered.

"I can go back to Craddock House," Misty suggested.

"We'll go with you," Clemmie said, motioning to Aunt Thelma.

"Okay, do you guys want to meet at our house later tonight for dinner?" I offered, looking at Vance.

"I think that's a good idea," he replied. "I have to run back to work, but you guys carry on and fill me in tonight."

We all agreed it was a plan.

Chapter 21

I hurried home to let Rocky out before heading to Silver Wand. Since the attack, he'd stayed inside a bit more, and I wanted to make sure he had plenty of time outside. As I pulled into my driveway, I noticed Jeremy's car pulling in at the same time next door. We got out and started talking.

"I'm surprised to see you here," I told him. "I thought you'd be at the hospital."

He looked at me with a mixture of confusion and surprise. "What do you mean? She's already home."

"What? I thought she just woke up this morning."

"She did," he said, shaking his head. "After I got home this morning and showered, I got a call from Dr. Fitz saying she was awake and asking for me.

When I got to the hospital, she was already sitting in bed, looking like she'd just awakened from a nap."

"They didn't need to keep her?"

"I guess not. I'm not complaining." Jeremy smiled. The expression lit up his entire face. I smiled in return. It felt good to see him happy. "She doesn't remember what happened, but Dr. Fitz thinks she just needs a bit of time. Do you want to talk to her?"

I was speechless for a moment. "I want to, but do you think it'll be too much?"

Jeremy laughed. "No, not at all."

I wasn't sure what to expect when we walked inside. I guess I thought Sarah would be sleeping or resting at least, but when we walked in, Sarah busy rearranging the furniture with her eyes darting around the room as if trying to find the perfect spot for each throw pillow. A vacuum cleaner was plugged in beside her.

She looked up when we walked in.

"This is Angelica, you know, the one who found you," Jeremy said by way of introduction.

"Angelica! It's so good to meet you!" she exclaimed, dropping what she was doing to hug me. "Thank you so much for everything. I don't know how to repay you." She held me at arm's length. Her voice was filled with warmth and genuine kindness.

"I'm just glad you're okay." I smiled, feeling a

sense of relief wash over me. I'd been worried Sarah wouldn't recover, and here she was, looking fit and healthy.

Sarah stepped back to look around the room. "I've got a lot of work to do, though. This place needs a serious makeover."

"I don't think she's going to let me rest until the house returns to its former glory," Jeremy joked. "Five years, must I remind you. You were gone for five years. I've been in survival mode."

Sarah rolled her eyes, but there was a twinkle in them that showed she was teasing. "Guess it's nice to know how much you love me."

Jeremy grinned and wrapped his arm around her, pulling her close and planting a kiss on her forehead.

"Thank you for loving me enough to wait for me," she said, leaning into him.

Jeremy held her close and smiled back. "Always," he said.

I smiled at the display of affection. They might still have some problems to work out, but it was clear that Sarah's return brought joy back into their lives.

I knew I said I would interview Caroline, but that was before I ran across Sarah. Her potential knowledge was too important to pass up.

"I know you don't remember anything from the attack, but what if I told you what I'd experienced from your point of view? Do you think it might help?"

Sarah stepped away from Jeremy. "I didn't know you'd experienced that." She looked apologetic.

"It's okay. It's how I found you," I explained.

"Why don't you sit down." Jeremy moved toward where I presumed the couch used to be before doing an about-face.

Sarah followed us to the makeshift sitting area. We all took a seat, and I began to recount the events that led to her discovery in the maze. She listened intently, nodding every now and then to let me know she was following along. When I finished, she looked at me with a mix of gratitude and confusion.

"I can't believe all that happened." She seemed to think her words through. "It seems vaguely familiar, but I still don't remember what I was doing there." Sarah looked disappointed.

I then thought of something. "Were you, by chance, working on a book? I remember you write true crime."

"I don't know. I could've been. I'm always working on a book," Sarah admitted.

"She's right. She always works."

"Where's my computer? Do you still have it?" Sarah asked Jeremy.

"I think it's in the office closet." Jeremy stood to retrieve it.

As we waited for the computer, I asked Sarah

more about her career. She told me she had written several books, including one about a small town in Maine with a haunted history.

"I've always been fascinated by the paranormal," she said, her eyes lighting up. "Why do ghosts stay here? Why don't they always cross over? I've interviewed some fascinating spirits over the years."

"I wonder if you were researching something to do with the Craddock House ghost?" I suggested.

"I very well could have been. It's honestly hard to say."

When Jeremy returned with the computer, and it was powered up and ready to go, Sarah immediately began searching through her files for any notes or drafts that might shed light on how she ended up at Craddock House.

Sarah navigated to her documents folder and pulled up a file. We all crowded around as she opened a file titled *Silverlake Secrets*.

"This is what I was working on that night," she said, turning the screen toward us.

It was a document with a list of names and artworks, along with notes about their history and value. At the top of the list was the name of a French painter, Jean-Luc Dubois.

"It looks like I was researching stolen artwork," Sarah explained. "This particular artist had a unique style that made his paintings valuable on the black market."

"You were looking at an impressionist painting when you were attacked. I remember it. It was a landscape with flowers, poppies, I think."

"Was this it?" Sarah searched for an image on her computer. Moments later, the painting from Craddock House appeared on the screen.

"Yes, that's it, but I don't remember still seeing it there last night, do you?" I asked Jeremy.

Jeremy studied the painting. "It doesn't look familiar, but I'm not sure."

"What's it called?" I asked.

Sarah looked back at her notes. "*Fields of Scarlet: A Summer Day in Provence.* It was stolen from a museum in Paris about eight years ago. They haven't been able to find it since."

"The thief must have hidden it in Craddock House," I said, putting the pieces together.

"They knew it was valuable and wanted to keep it safe until they could sell it on the black market," Sarah agreed.

"How did you track it to Craddock House?" I asked.

Sarah scrolled through her notes. "I don't know. It's not written down." Sarah continued to read her research. "Does the name Louisa Garnier ring any bells?" She looked up at me.

Yes, it did, and for a moment, I couldn't remember why. Then it clicked into place. "Louisa

Garnier is Luella Morgan's sister. She's been living in France for the past twenty years."

"I think you mean to say she's been stealing paintings in France for twenty years." Sarah brought up a red notice from Interpol.

Red Notice: Louisa Garnier

Louisa Garnier is wanted for questioning concerning the theft of several valuable pieces of artwork, including paintings by the French artists Jean-Luc Dubois, Pauline Beaumont, and Simon Moreau. Garnier has been linked to several high-profile art heists in France, Italy, and Spain and is believed to have been involved in the black market sale of stolen artwork. Any information regarding her whereabouts should be reported to local authorities immediately. Garnier should be considered armed and dangerous.

I asked Sarah to search for information on Luella Morgan or Elle Raven, but nothing came up.

"It looks like Garnier is the only one on their radar," Sarah said.

"I wonder if Luella knows what her sister's up to or if she's in on it," I questioned out loud.

"Without any evidence, it's hard to say," Sarah remarked.

Well, then, it looked like it was time to gather some evidence.

I DIALED Sheriff Reynolds when I got into my house, eager to tell him about the stolen paintings and the possible connection between Louisa Garnier and Luella Morgan. Dottie answered the phone with her usual chipper tone. "Sheriff's office, how can I help you today?"

"Dottie, it's Angelica. I need to speak to Sheriff Reynolds right away," I said, urgency creeping into my voice.

"Well, hello, Angelica. How lovely to hear from you. Isn't it just a gorgeous day out? I swear, I could sit out there all day and just soak up the sun," Dottie gushed, oblivious to the seriousness of my call.

"Dottie, please, this is important. I need to speak with the sheriff about a stolen painting and a possible suspect." I tried to keep my frustration in check.

"Oh, I'm sorry, hun. The sheriff's in a meeting with Dr. Fitz. He specifically asked me not to disturb him, but I'll tell him you called as soon as he's out. Is there anything else I can help you with?"

"No, that's all. Thank you," I replied, hanging up the phone and taking a deep breath. As much as I wanted to head to the gallery with my wand drawn and ready to demand answers, I knew that was a dumb move. If Elle was involved with her sister, that could backfire on me. Instead, I hoped the sheriff would call me back soon, and we could question Elle together.

But that didn't mean I had to sit around and do nothing. I was torn between interviewing Caroline and checking in on Mrs. Potts. Caroline might remember someone working at the house who could've helped fence the stolen paintings, or perhaps she could've been an accomplice, not that I could see her doing that. Caroline was a sweet old lady, but I didn't want to rule the prospect out, either. I've learned to expect the unexpected when it comes to solving crimes.

Mrs. Potts, on the other hand, was working with Elle now, and if she were fencing stolen goods, Mrs. Potts might have information and not even realize it. In the end, I decided to visit Mrs. Potts.

Chapter 22

When I approached Mrs. Potts' front door, I heard voices drifting from the backyard. It sounded like Mrs. Potts was enjoying some friendly conversation with Mrs. Thomas, who lived next door. I decided to head around to the backyard to see if I could catch Mrs. Potts for a quick chat.

As I rounded the corner of the house, I saw two figures sitting in lawn chairs, sipping iced tea and chatting animatedly. Mrs. Potts was there, but the other figure was not Mrs. Thomas. Instead, it was Elle. My pace faltered, and I dashed behind a magnolia bush before they could see me. It wasn't the best hiding spot, but I needed to disappear somewhere fast where I could transform into Penelope.

I had my fingers wrapped around my amulet, ready to say the incantation, when Elle raised her wand out of nowhere and blasted Mrs. Potts with an unknown spell. A purple cloud of smoke enveloped her face. I was frozen in shock.

"Will you quit doing that?" Heidi said, stepping out onto the back porch from inside the house. "She's going to end up in a madhouse if you keep flicking your wand in her face."

"It's not my fault she uncovered the truth. The old woman is smarter than I remembered."

"Old woman? She's your age," Heidi retorted.

"Hush your mouth," Elle snapped back.

Mrs. Potts stood up and shuffled her feet forward toward a rose bush. She slowly bent forward and smelled the bloom. Her movements aged her, all because of whatever spell Elle had used on her. I needed to backtrack and call the sheriff immediately.

"Oh, hello. Who are you?"

I looked up and right into Mrs. Potts's eyes. I was a sitting duck. "H-h-hi, Mrs. Potts," I said, coming around the corner.

"Oh, Angelica, we didn't see you there," Elle said. A perfect fake smile etched onto her face. Heidi's expression matched hers. It was startling how wicked these women were.

"Sorry, I didn't mean to sneak up on you. I heard voices and thought I'd come back and say hi." I took out my cell phone and shot off a group text. It read *911. Mrs. Potts' house.* That should be enough to send the calvary charging. At least, I hoped it would.

"Would you like some iced tea?" Elle offered.

My eyes followed Mrs. Potts as she walked around her yard, examining everything like she saw it for the first time.

"She's having a bad day," Heidi said, following my line of sight.

Only because you're messing with her memory, I thought. The entire ordeal made my blood boil. I wanted nothing more than to blast both women on their backsides. I didn't know all the details of their scheme, but it was clear they were up to no good, and they had been at it for some time.

"No, that's okay. I can come back and visit some other time."

"Nonsense. We won't hear of such things. It'd do Dorothy a world of good to have a friend to talk to, isn't that right?" Elle said the second part louder so Mrs. Potts could hear. The poor woman ignored her and continued to shuffle around her yard. I felt sick to my stomach.

"How are you today?" I played the part, walking over to Mrs. Potts and rubbing her shoulder.

"Oh, hello, who are you?" she asked, repeating the exact phrase from moments ago. Her eyes were cloudy, and her skin felt cold and clammy even though it was a warm spring day. This wasn't right.

I needed to get Mrs. Potts out of here. She needed help.

"Do you want to take a walk, Mrs. Potts?" I suggested.

"A walk. Do I like walks?"

"I think you do. We can walk up and down the sidewalk." In fact, I'd walk her right to my car and get us the heck out of there. The sheriff could deal with arresting these women. I steered Mrs. Potts toward the front of the house. "Come on, let's go."

"Are you okay? You're acting awfully suspicious," Elle confronted me as I encouraged Mrs. Potts to keep moving.

I instinctively took two steps back. "Hmm? Why would you say that? I'm just worried about Mrs. Potts," I lied. "Don't you think a walk would be a good idea?"

Elle didn't answer me. She was looking at Heidi. "What do you think, the last fifteen minutes?" she said.

"Are you sure that's a good idea?" Heidi looked unsure.

"Of course, I'm sure. Look at her. She knows something." Elle eyed me with hawk-like precision.

"I don't like this," Heidi replied. I had to agree with Heidi; I didn't like this either, and I had no idea what was going on.

"You don't have to like it. You just have to do as I say." Elle drew her wand.

"You're not going to do anything," I bit back, taking out my wand.

"Oh! Is this a play? I love the theater!" Mrs. Potts clapped her hands.

"Is that so?" Elle replied with a smug expression.

I knew I had to act fast. I dodged to the left just as a shot of blue light whizzed past my head. I responded with one of my own. We volleyed curses back and forth, each one narrowly missing its intended target.

This wasn't my first face-off with a psychotic witch. Luckily, I had plenty of practice. At that moment, I drew on my past training and remembered a bubble charm my friend Luke had taught me this past winter. I quickly deployed it, creating a shimmering force field around Mrs. Potts and me. I tried to keep her safely tucked behind me as the duel continued.

Heidi stood on the sidelines and watched Elle and I exchange spells. I took the opportunity to try and reason with her. "Heidi, you don't have to be part of this. You can help me stop Elle and bring an end to this."

Heidi looked conflicted.

But Elle interrupted, sending a curse at me that shattered the bubble charm. I quickly cast another spell to protect us, but I knew I couldn't keep it up for long. The situation was escalating quickly.

"Heidi, please, help me," I said, shooting off a defensive freezing charm.

Heidi bit her bottom lip.

"Heidi Ann Morgan, don't listen to her. I brought you into this world, and I can take you out of it!" Elle shouted.

You know the sound a record makes when the needle slides across it? That sound played in my head. "What did you just say?" I asked while reinforcing the bubble charm, but Elle didn't answer. She continued talking to her daughter, commanding her to do as she was told.

"Kill this witch, and let's put an end to this!" Elle demanded.

That snapped Heidi out of it. She stood up straighter; her wand pointed at her mother. "No, Mom," she said firmly. "Angelica is a good person, and what you're doing is wrong."

Elle turned her attention to Heidi, her eyes blazing with fury. "How dare you even think about betraying me. Do you want to spend the rest of your life in prison?"

Heidi's face twisted in agony as she looked back and forth between her mother and me. "I can't do this anymore," she said, her voice quivering. "I'm tired of doing everything I'm told and protecting your secrets."

Elle's expression darkened. "You're throwing everything away," she said, her voice low and menacing. "All for what? To protect some witch you don't even know. You're making a big mistake."

"Your threats won't work on me anymore. I won't live like this." Heidi's voice grew stronger.

Elle's eyes flashed with anger. "Don't you dare talk back to me! You will do as you're told or regret it for the rest of your life."

Heidi ignored her and turned to me. "See this woman right here? She killed her sister. That's why she ran away. She killed her sister and assumed her identity, living in Paris as Louisa Garnier."

"Why you!" Elle fired off a curse at her daughter, but she was ready for it and hit her mother with a stunning spell. Elle had been too blind with rage to even react. "Then she forced me to live with her lies, grooming me to do her bidding. I grew up in fear!" Heidi's voice shook. "Fear that she'd kill me like she'd killed my aunt if I didn't do as she said." Heidi turned and spoke directly to her mother. "But I'm not afraid of you anymore. You have no power over me!" Her voice rang out as her mother was magically stunned into silence.

"It was you who broke into our garage apartment?" I surmised, looking at Heidi clearly for the first time.

"It was. I'm so sorry."

"What about Sarah? Did you curse her?"

Tears streamed down Heidi's face, and I knew I had my answer.

"She would've killed me if I hadn't."

"And Harriet? Did she know the truth?"

Heidi nodded. "Mom paid her money to keep her quiet all these years. Said it was for the best. Harriet's husband couldn't hold a job."

"There'd never been a baking contest."

Heidi seemed confused. Her mother never thought to share the lie she'd told me explaining Harriet's note.

I felt a mix of anger and empathy wash over me; anger that Heidi had been manipulated and forced to do something she never wanted to do and compassion for the fear she must have felt all these years.

As the sirens grew louder in the distance, the effects of Elle's stunning charm started to wear off. Just as I moved to subdue Elle, Mrs. Potts reached into her pocket and withdrew a wand. Without missing a beat, she pointed it at Elle and shouted, "Potentia exuo!"

A blinding light erupted from Mrs. Potts' wand, illuminating the garden. The light swirled around Elle, enveloping her in a tornado of magic. The winds pulled strands of colors from Elle one by one like she was making cotton candy. Vibrant pink, fiery red, lime green, pastel lavender, and rich blue blended, creating a swirling mass of power, which then shot up in the air and exploded like a firework on the Fourth of July. I shielded my eyes from the brightness, unsure of what was happening.

When it was all said and done, Elle stood there stunned, glowing like a mere mortal. I realized then that Mrs. Potts had stripped Elle of her powers. The witch was no longer a threat.

"I don't know who she is, but I don't like her," Mrs. Potts muttered, still as confused as ever. I closed my eyes and shook my head. Even with her mind scrambled, Mrs. Potts was still one of my favorite people.

As we made our way toward the front of the house with Elle held at wand point, I could see the flashing lights of multiple patrol cars pulling up outside. I felt a sense of relief that the situation was finally ending but also a sense of sadness for Heidi. She had been a victim of her mother's schemes for far too long. Not to mention Sarah; five years of her life had been wasted. And what about Louisa? I still didn't understand why Luella had killed her sister.

There'd be time for answers later. Right now, I was just happy the threat was neutralized.

"I was just going to call you," the sheriff said, exiting his patrol car. "What'd you do to her?" He motioned to Elle.

"Not sure. Mrs. Potts took her down."

The sheriff nodded as if that explained it. "I was talking with Dr. Fitz. That DNA test? The one from Lily? He decided to process it after someone tried breaking in. More on a hunch than anything. Turns out, it matched the remains." Fifteen minutes ago, that knowledge would've surprised me, but now, it was just more evidence to lock Elle away for a long, long time.

Chapter 23

I was jolted awake by a cold breeze that seemed to pass right through me and the sense that someone was watching me. It was the same feeling I'd experienced last week when the Craddock House ghost woke me. I sat up slowly in bed and looked around the room, trying to see if she were here with us now. I didn't see anyone, but I could feel her presence. Vance was asleep on his side, turned away from me, and seemed to be sleeping peacefully. I let him be as I slipped out of bed and walked softly to the window. That's when I saw her standing in the garden under the giant oak tree and looking straight at me.

I held up my index finger, signaling I'd be down in a minute. Hopefully, the sign was a universal gesture.

I slipped out of the backdoor, feeling chilled by

the early morning air. The grass was dewy and cold under my feet as I made my way to the garden. She was still waiting there for me. I took that as a good sign. When I approached her, the woman slowly turned to face me, her ghostly form flickering in the dim light of dawn.

"Thank you," she whispered, her voice barely audible.

"For what?" I asked. I had my suspicions, but I needed her to confirm them.

"For bringing my killer to justice," she replied. "I've been trapped in this state for so long, unable to speak or communicate with anyone, but now, thanks to you, I can finally rest in peace."

"You're Louisa."

"I am."

"I don't understand. Why did your sister kill you?"

Louisa's ghost spoke in a soft voice, revealing her tragic story. "She killed me because I found out about her double life. She was an art thief, even back then. She was tired of being poor. She thought she would never make it as an artist, no matter how much we insisted she was talented."

I nodded, encouraging Louisa to continue.

"The night I died, I discovered a painting in her apartment. The gallery in town had gotten in an original Dubois. It was a huge deal. When I found out Luella stole it and replaced it with a forgery, I confronted her. We argued, and things got out of hand. She struck me with a nearby vase, and I fell to the floor, never to get up again."

"The bloodstain in the apartment is from you."

Louisa nodded. "I wanted to tell you. I wanted to tell anyone and everyone, but Luella cursed me. I couldn't speak, act, or do anything that would bring her crimes to light, but you changed all that."

I felt a chill run down my spine as Louisa's story sank in. It was a tragic end for a talented artist and her sister, who had only wanted to help her. "I'm so sorry," I said, the words feeling inadequate. "I wish I could have helped you sooner."

"You did help me. You brought my killer to justice, and now, I can rest in peace, knowing the truth has been revealed." Louisa smiled at me. "I'm free now," she said, her voice stronger than ever. Tears streamed down my face as I watched her slowly disappear. I felt a sense of closure, knowing I had helped bring justice to Louisa.

As I turned to walk back inside, I felt a weight lifted off my shoulders. The sun was just beginning to rise, and the world was waking up around me. It was a new day, and I was ready to face whatever it had in store for me.

THE FOLLOWING DAY WAS SATURDAY. It was my day to meet Misty for coffee and conversation at her bookshop. Given the past week, we had plenty to catch up on.

As I walked into Spellbinding Books, I was surprised to see Mrs. Potts and Clemmie chatting away in the romance section. They were sitting shoulder to shoulder at a small table with a laptop open in front of them.

"Angelica, dear, it's so lovely to see you," she said, standing and giving me a warm hug. "I'm told you're to thank for giving me my life back."

"Oh, I don't know about that," I started to say. Truth be told, I was just happy to see Mrs. Potts back to her old self again.

"Hush now, she's just being modest," Clemmie said to Mrs. Potts. "Dorothy is right. Without you, she'd have been declared coo-coo by the end of the week."

I grimaced.

"Don't I know it. I recognized Elle as Luella that moment I laid eyes on her. I didn't think anything of it until I spotted several copies of the same painting at her house. She was making forgeries! I opened my mouth before I thought better of it, and POOF! Memory erased. What a horrible woman."

"I'm so sorry that happened to you," I replied.

"That's what I get for paying her a social visit.

What if her spell was irreversible?" Mrs. Potts asked.

I didn't want to think about that.

"We're all thankful it was," Clemmie said.

I agreed and promptly changed the subject. If I played the game of *what if* much longer, I'd probably start to cry. I cleared my throat. "What are you two ladies up to?"

"I'm setting up her online dating profile. What does it look like we're doing?" Clemmie said with a twinkle in her eye.

Mrs. Potts blushed, clearly embarrassed by the attention.

"Are you sure that's a good idea? Nothing good ever comes from online dating," I declared.

Clemmie shushed me. "If only Vance's granddaddy lived in town, he'd save us some trouble." I laughed. Vance's grandfather was a handsome man and single, but he lived in Tampa. "But seeing as he doesn't, we've got work to do."

"Okay, just be safe." I felt like I was talking to a couple of teenagers. "Are you still talking to the same man?" I asked Clemmie.

"Which one?"

"Clemmie! You have that many suitors?"

"What? You've got the play the field. I'm not about to settle at my age."

"Mm-hmm," Mrs. Potts agreed with her.

"But just so you know, I'm thinking of inviting

Boyfriend Number Three to Silverlake next month for Thelma's party." Clemmie smiled.

"Really?" Mrs. Potts and I asked at the same time.

"Really. Just wait until you meet him."

Oh boy, I wasn't sure if this was going to be a good thing or a bad thing.

Misty walked over. "Do you think we should have a safety seminar for online dating for seniors?" I asked my best friend.

"Nah, we covered the basics, right, Clemmie?" Clemmie didn't hear Misty. She was too busy getting Mrs. Potts the rundown on her dating profile. "Besides, how much trouble can they get into?" Misty asked.

"Are you kidding me? Plenty." And I had a feeling we would soon find out.

WHAT'S NEXT? **Fatal Enchantment**

Stephanie Damore Complete Works

MYSTIC INN MYSTERIES
Witchy Reservations
Eerie Check In
Spooked Solid
Untimely Departure
Midnight at Mystic Inn
Bewitch Break Inn
Potions, Poison, and Pumpkin Spice
Jingle Bells and Wedding Spells
Spellbinding Secrets
Fatal Enchantment

. . .

SPIRITED SWEETS MYSTERIES
Bittersweet Betrayal

Decadent Demise

Red Velvet Revenge

Sugared Suspect

WITCH IN TIME
Better Witch Next Time

Play for Time

Time Will Tell

BEAUTY SECRETS SERIES
Makeup & Murder

Kiss & Makeup

Eyeliner & Alibis

Pedicures & Prejudice

Beauty & Bloodshed

Charm & Deception

A DROP DEAD *Famous Cozy Mystery*
Mourning After

About the Author

Stephanie Damore is a USA Today bestselling mystery author known for her fun and fearless stories featuring smart and sassy sleuths. With a soft spot for magic and romance, Damore's books are perfect for readers who enjoy a dash of romance and a twist of whodunit.

For information on new releases and fun give-aways, visit her Facebook group: Paranormal Mystery Coven

www.facebook.com/groups/
paranormalcozymystery/

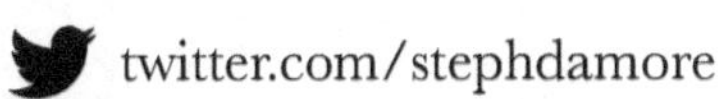 twitter.com/stephdamore

instagram.com/steph_damore_author

bookbub.com/profile/stephanie-damore

www.ingramcontent.com/pod-product-compliance
Lightning Source LLC
Chambersburg PA
CBHW030934210726
48290CB00007B/2182